MISSIN

Light from a passing car glinted off something metallic half-buried in the thick shrubbery behind Esme's garage. Alicia hurried over to get a better look.

"Quinn!" she screamed a second later. "It's here. It's Nicole's bike. I'd know it anywhere."

Alicia wheeled the bike out of the bushes. It was blue with a white seat and white tape around the handlebars. "Quinn, she *has* been here." Alicia sounded amazed.

Quinn's face was set in a serious expression. "And she lost this in the process." Quinn pulled a yellow "I love LaLa Land" scarf off a branch where it was snagged.

Looking at the scarf, Alicia slowly shook her head. "Oh, Quinn," she wailed. "Something awful's happened to Nicole. I feel it, here." She tapped her heart emphatically with one finger, as a few tears trickled down her cheeks.

Quinn wanted to tell Alicia she was overreacting, but she couldn't. A terrible thought had just occurred to her. "Lish, I'm worried. Nicole's family is very rich and, well, very high society. Maybe she's been kidnapped . . ."

LONELY HEART

Developed by

Elle Wolfe

LONELY HEART

Cover art by Richard Lester

ISBN: 1-55902-985-4

First edition: August 1990

Printed in the United States of America

0 9 8 7 6 5 4 3 2 1

For Northsky

LONELY HEART

CHAPTER 1

"Esme Farrell!" Nicole Whitcomb scolded into the phone. "Stop it! I will not wear your Mickey Mouse ears out to dinner!" Then, she giggled.

The line crackled as a loud clap of thunder made the house tremble slightly. It was a rainy December evening in Palm Beach, Florida. Outside Nicole's second-floor bedroom window, the wind bent the tall palm trees low toward the ground. It was the kind of night that made Nicole want to stay home and gossip with her friends on the phone. It was definitely not a night to get dressed up in her very best clothes and go out to dinner in one of the town's fanciest restaurants. But, like it or not, Nicole was stuck with going out. And not just with her mother, but with her mom's latest boyfriend, Adam Stanton. Nicole called him "the Mouse."

Nicole hated complaining to anyone, even to her best friend, Esme, but she didn't like the idea of this dumb dinner, rain or no rain. Her best friend was definitely trying to make her feel better—her three best friends, really. Her other two best friends, Quinn McNair and Alicia Antona, were over at Esme's helping her cram for a make-up math exam. They were all in the sixth grade class at Palm Beach Prep together. Nicole heard them arguing about some song over Esme's giggling.

"Hold on a minute, Nicole," Esme instructed, after she stopped laughing. Nicole could hear her yelling at Quinn and Alicia. "You guys, be quiet! I'm on the phone here!"

Quinn answered, just as loudly. "Ooooh!" she teased. "We're sooo sorry."

Then Esme was back. "Alicia wants to know what the Mouse is like."

"Is he handsome?" Alicia demanded.

"With a nickname like that?" Quinn scoffed back, louder than before, if that was possible.

"He's not anything like your dad, is he, Nicole?" Esme asked.

Nicole drew in her breath sharply. She glanced up at the photo of her father taped to the mirror. "No, he's not at all like my dad," she said in a small voice, and then, cleared her throat. "He really *is* kind of a mouse. He's bald, for one thing." She giggled, picturing the shiny wide dome of Adam Stanton's head. "And he's always saying, 'God only created so many perfect heads, the rest he covered with hair.' It drives me crazy!"

Esme chuckled. "Hold on a sec." Nicole heard her relay the Mouse's comment to Alicia and Quinn. They both cracked up.

"Well, they liked it, Nicole," Esme said when she got back on the phone.

Nicole was quiet for a moment. "He's from New York, and raises money for charities. That's how they met. Last spring my mother helped organize that big National Homeless Drive, and he was in charge of fund-raising." As she talked, she swung her phone's long blue extension cord round and round, like a jump rope. Nicole's mother was always arranging benefits and fund-raisers to help people. She never spent that much time at home and, for the most part, Nicole's grandparents, the Todds, had brought her up. Mrs. Whitcomb had some pretty important friends, but Nicole thought they were really boring.

Adam wasn't at all like her mother's other friends, who were all pretty important. And he definitely wasn't glamorous. Nicole tried to think what it was about him that bothered her, but she'd never put it into words before. "He's sort of—well, boring." Even as she said it, she knew that wasn't really the case. At least he wasn't boring in the way that the pretty important friends were. He just wasn't, well, like her father. "I don't really know what she sees in him!" she finished.

"Do you think they're serious?" Esme asked, concerned.

"Esme!" Nicole cried, horrified. "What makes you think a thing like that? Mom's dated lots of people. She's never been serious before."

"Yeah, but I never remember her dating any one person for this long before—or taking you out to dinner," Esme responded.

Nicole sighed. "That's true." She tried to ease the queasy feeling in her stomach. Lately, every time her mother mentioned Adam's name, Nicole got that feeling in her stomach. She never really paid any attention to the men her mother had dated after her parents' divorce six years ago. Not until now. Adam Stanton *was* around quite often, and her mother *did* spend a lot of time in New York, where he lived.

"Your mother doesn't know that you think he's a mouse, does she?" Esme asked curiously, bringing Nicole back to the present.

Nicole frowned. "Of course not." It never occurred to her to talk to her mother about Adam. "Besides," Nicole continued, shrugging, "she doesn't care what I think. If she did care what I thought about him, she'd ask me." Nicole shifted the receiver from her right hand to her left, and buttoned and unbuttoned the top button of her yellow drop-waist dress. She stuck her tongue out at her reflection in the mirror. "I should just put on jeans," Nicole said. "Then I couldn't go to dinner with them at the Breakers. Besides, I hate dressing up more than anything."

Tossing her shoulder-length brown hair out of her eyes, and reaching for a yellow hair-ribbon, Nicole practiced looking angry in the mirror. She squinted her big brown eyes into two slits, but the result was disappointing. Instead of looking angry that she was being dragged along on one of her mother's dates, she looked as if she'd swallowed a lemon.

"I wouldn't let the Mouse spoil my dinner, if I were you," Esme advised. "I mean, you are going to the Breakers, after all!" She sounded a little disgusted with her oldest friend. "And dressing up is the best part of going out. Sometimes, I just don't think you're normal!" Esme had a hard time understanding Nicole's lack of enthusiasm for clothes. Esme was a teen model and her life *was* clothes. Nicole actually liked her Palm Beach Prep uniform because then she didn't have to worry about what to wear every day.

"Maybe that's the problem!" Nicole exclaimed. "Maybe I'm not normal!" She sighed as she poked her head into her closet, trying to locate her good black flats. She picked up an old pair of riding boots, and sighed again. "I'd rather be down at the stables with Candy's mare than going out to dinner—with anybody. . . ."

"Horses!" Esme snorted. "You always bring horses into everything!"

"I do not!" Nicole retorted. "Well . . . not all the time," she amended. "I just don't want to miss being with the vet when Ginger foals. And he did say it should be some time this week. But . . ." Nicole never got to finish her sentence because of the commotion on the other end of the line.

"Can you hang on a minute, Nicole?" Esme asked as she put the receiver down on the floor.

Nicole heard Quinn and Alicia screaming goodbye. Then, there was silence.

A little while later, Esme was back on the phone. Nicole took the interruption as an opportunity to change the subject. "Have you heard from your agent yet about that big modeling job down in the Florida Keys over the holidays, Es?"

Esme sighed deeply into the phone. "Nope. Not yet. I mean, nothing definite. The shoot starts this weekend, but even if I get the job I probably wouldn't start working until the week after Christmas. *During* vacation," she added, sounding particularly tragic.

"That's just two weeks from now!" Nicole exclaimed. "Come on, you'll have a great time. Besides," Nicole suddenly remembered, "if you went to the Keys before school was out, you'd miss our Christmas play!"

Esme laughed. "I hadn't thought about that. Imagine not being in a Christmas performance together. That would be a first for us."

Nicole suddenly felt choked up. "If you hadn't been such an airhead and lost your myrrh back when we were in the kindergarten play together, we might never have been friends."

"Oh, I would have figured some way to wheedle my way into your life, even if I'm not on Palm Beach's *Social Register*!" Esme said, chuckling mischievously. Teasing Nicole about her prestigious "old Palm Beach" family was one of Esme's favorite occupations. "Besides, if I didn't turn up to star in Quinn McNair's very first play, I think she'd kill me."

"Alicia, too," Nicole reminded her. "Senorita Antona is really excited about being director."

Before Esme could respond, Nicole's mother called from downstairs. "Nicole darling, are you ready?"

"Ooops, I've got to go!" Nicole announced.

"See ya' later. And have a good time—or pretend to," Esme suggested before hanging up.

Nicole took a deep breath to steady her queasy stomach. Her mother's voice had brought Adam Stanton back into her life.

"Nicole? We've got to go. Adam called. He

can't pick us up and we have to meet him in fifteen minutes."

"Coming!" Nicole answered, and hastily pulled her hair back off her face into a ponytail and tied it with the yellow ribbon. She started out of her room, and got as far as the stairs before stopping short.

"Nicole, where are you going?" Diana Whitcomb asked, annoyed.

"I forgot my purse," Nicole replied, as she ducked back into her room—her purse already hanging from her shoulder. She went over to her dresser and planted a kiss on her father's taped-up picture. It was a photo she had clipped from the latest issue of *National Geographic.* Standing on the prow of his ship, the *Starry Night,* his light brown hair ruffled by the wind, Christopher Whitcomb looked every inch the famous scientist/explorer he was. "Love you!" Nicole whispered, before she hurried back out of her room and down the sweeping front staircase of the old Todd mansion.

CHAPTER 2

"I hope nothing happened to Adam!" Mrs. Whitcomb exclaimed, as she twisted and untwisted her pink linen napkin. For the third time in as many minutes, she checked her watch and then actually sighed. She smiled distractedly at Nicole and then peered out from under her brown, blunt-cut bangs toward the entrance of the Breakers's famous Circle Dining Room.

Nicole stared at her mother in horrid fascination. Why was she making such a big deal about Adam being a few minutes late? It was nothing to get so crazy about. And why was she so dressed up? It was only a weeknight—and it was only Adam. Mrs. Whitcomb was wearing a black shift dress with tiny gold threads that made the gold flecks in her big brown eyes positively sparkle. Her mother almost looked like she was seventeen and still in high school. The thought bothered Nicole as she looked around the crowded dining room. She half-expected someone from one of those corny television commercials to walk up and say, "Hey, you two look like sisters." Because they did look like sisters—only a few years apart.

And now, her mother was falling to pieces, just because her date was ten minutes late. The woman who was used to giving speeches at charity balls was reduced to a quivering mass of nerves. Nicole was embarrassed for her. It was just some guy, after all.

"Mother, *nothing* happened to him. He probably just got tied up," Nicole reassured her mother, not understanding why this dinner with Adam Stanton was such a big deal anyway. They must have had a million dinners together. "Besides, looking so upset because your date is ten minutes late is definitely very uncool."

Diana Whitcomb gave Nicole a withering look. "I'm afraid it's your language these days that's 'uncool.' You're changing in ways I do not approve of," her mother said in her best hoity-toity upper-crust Palm Beach voice. Then she paused ever so slightly before adding quietly, "You're beginning to sound like that Nueva Beach friend of yours, Casey—"

"Quinn," Nicole interrupted. Her mother's snobbish attitude about Quinn made her sick.

Quinn McNair was a scholarship student at PBP, and Nicole didn't understand why her mother had such bad feelings about her newest friend. Because the McNairs lived in Nueva Beach, a decidedly lower- to middle-class neighborhood, Mrs. Whitcomb had forbidden Nicole to visit her house—a rule Nicole had been breaking a lot lately. But, even though Mrs. Whitcomb had this thing against Quinn, she didn't really care what Nicole was doing—or not doing. And that bothered Nicole more than whatever her mother had against Quinn.

Nicole's cheeks turned pink. She wanted to ask her mother how she knew she'd changed since they hardly spent any time together. But she bit her tongue and defended Quinn instead. "Quinn McNair's her name, and you're bound to be hearing a lot of it one day, Mom. She's already won a statewide writing contest and she's only twelve and . . ."

Nicole broke off because some loud voices over by the maître d' caught her attention. She turned around to see what was happening. "Oh!" Nicole exclaimed. "I think you're going to wish that the Mouse had never showed up." Adam's nickname slipped right out, and Nicole clapped her hand over her mouth. But Mrs. Whitcomb didn't even notice.

Adam Stanton had certainly arrived. And with him was a boy who looked about thirteen or fourteen. He was wearing a leather bomber jacket, and very faded jeans. It was obvious that the maître d' was trying to convince Adam that the boy couldn't come into the restaurant—dressed the way he was.

"Now why in the world did Adam bring him?" Mrs. Whitcomb murmured, and then looked quickly at Nicole. She smiled a thin version of her best old-family Palm Beach smile. "I'll be right back," she said to her daughter. Then she pushed back her chair and started across the room.

A moment later, she was at the door, planting a light kiss on Adam Stanton's cheek. She extended a hand to the boy and actually smiled at him. Then, hooking her arm through Adam's, she guided him back toward their table. The boy and maître d' followed.

"Nicole, I don't believe you've met Jonathan, Adam's son," Mrs. Whitcomb said smoothly, taking her seat.

"Uh—no, I haven't," Nicole stuttered and gulped. She stared at Jonathan, especially at his left ear. He was wearing a small gold hoop-earring. She had never met a guy with an earring before, at least not a boy so near her own age. Some of Quinn's brother Sean's friends had earrings, but they were a lot older, like in high school. Jonathan only seemed to be a little older than she was.

"Hello," she managed to say, very shyly. Jonathan didn't seem to be too friendly—even if he was good-looking. She had a feeling Esme and Alicia would go crazy over him, with his longish dark curly hair, earring, and leather jacket.

He just grunted at her, and then plopped down into his chair, sprawling as he landed. Beneath his jacket, he was wearing a Terence Trent D'Arby T-shirt, just like the one Alicia had bought Quinn at his Fort Lauderdale concert last week. It was black with TTD's name scrawled in blood-red letters.

Adam glowered at his son, who glowered back, and then smiled at Nicole. "Glad to see you could make it, Nicky."

Nicole sat up straighter. This whole situation was getting out-of-hand. "I prefer being called Nicole, Mr. Stanton," she said in her best upper-crust voice, imitating her grandmother perfectly.

Out of the corner of her eye, Nicole saw Jonathan lift one eyebrow. Something about that reminded her of Quinn.

" 'Mr. Stanton'?" Adam asked, confused. He looked from Nicole to her mother, and then back to Nicole.

Mrs. Whitcomb cleared her throat. "As I told you this morning, Nicole, you can call Adam by his first name. He'd prefer that, I think." She stopped and gave him a soft look, which almost made Nicole sick. Her mother added, "And so would I." Her eyes pleaded with her daughter to make this difficult situation easier.

Nicole suddenly felt bad. "Okay," she gave in quickly. "I'm just not used to calling my mother's friends by their first names."

Adam smiled and let out a relieved sigh. "Now, I guess I'd better explain about Jonathan."

Jonathan sat back in his chair and folded his arms across his chest. He looked at the Mouse as if whatever he was about to say would be extremely interesting. Then, he leaned forward, and asked curiously, "Are you going to start with my current situation?"

Nicole was surprised to find Jonathan suddenly staring intently at her. "I'd say congratulations are in order, wouldn't you?" Nicole just stared back blankly. "I've just gotten the boot from the third prep school in two years," he informed her, and then lifted Nicole's water glass to toast himself.

Nicole's eyes widened. She'd never met anyone who had been kicked out of school, let alone someone who was proud of it.

Jonathan laughed at her surprise, and leaned back again, this time tilting his chair so far that it rested on only two legs. After a sharp glance from his father, he straightened his chair again, the front two legs hitting the floor with a resounding clunk. Mrs. Whitcomb began to look a bit embarrassed.

"It's nothing to brag about!" the Mouse reprimanded, shoving his glasses back up on his nose and glaring at his son.

"Not bragging," Jonathan mumbled. "Just telling the truth." He leaned on his elbows and addressed Nicole. "You look like perfect little Miss Prep School yourself. What grade are you in?" he asked.

"Nicole goes to Palm Beach Prep," Mrs. Whitcomb answered for her daughter, before Nicole had a chance to open her mouth.

Nicole shot her mother an annoyed glance, and answered for herself, "I'm in sixth grade."

"Palm Beach Prep, as I understand it, is the sister school to G. Adams Prep, no?" Adam asked Nicole, motioning for the waiter to bring the menus.

"Uh—yes," Nicole stuttered, squirming in her seat. No other boyfriend of her mother's had ever asked her about school before. In fact, no other boyfriend of her mother's had asked her about anything. Maybe Alicia was right. Maybe her mother was getting serious about this little man.

"Way cool!" Jonathan exclaimed, grinning. "G. Adams is my new prison, and now that you'll be my sister . . ."

"Your what?!" Nicole asked, her head jerking up. She stared right at Jonathan and then at her mother. He mother, blushing to her hairline, wouldn't meet her eyes. It was a dead giveaway.

"Mom?" Nicole squeaked, barely getting the word out. Adam took her mother's hand. For a moment, Nicole felt as if she was in a wind tunnel. All she heard was the thumping of her own heart, and, very faintly, the jazzed-up version of "Santa Claus Is Coming to Town" that the dance band was playing in the next room.

Nicole's mother started to explain. Nicole held her breath. She knew what was coming, but it couldn't really be happening. Under the table, she pinched the back of her hand, hard. It hurt. She wasn't in the middle of a bad dream. She was, unfortunately, very wide-awake.

"We didn't want to tell you like this," Diana Whitcomb began to explain, giving Jonathan a scathing glance.

He just grinned and shrugged.

She took a deep breath, and continued, "We decided to get married over the Christmas holiday. It'll be a small reception at home for just our friends and family. So Jonathan will be your brother—stepbrother. And Adam will be your stepfather, of course."

Nicole couldn't believe the way her mother had added that bit at the end about Adam, almost like it didn't really matter. As if getting a stepfather was no big deal. Who was her mother trying to kid?

"You're really getting married?" Nicole asked, feeling stupid. But she had to hear it just one more time, to be sure it was really happening. "To *him*?" She just couldn't believe it. She looked from Adam to her mother.

Adam and her mother both smiled at her. "That's why we're out tonight, to celebrate. *Together*," Adam said, stressing the last word slightly.

"So now we can be one big, happy family," Jonathan added, a little sourly. Nicole looked at him sharply. He seemed to be as unhappy about this wedding as she was. Nicole wondered if he had lived with his mother until now.

Nicole's mother must have seen that her daughter didn't look as happy as she should. "I know this is sudden for you, darling," she began, "but we're both sure this is the right thing for us. We'll all just have to adjust to one another. And that's going to take time. But Adam is moving down here, so you won't have to change schools or anything."

"And this wedding suited my mother just fine," Jonathan said sarcastically. "She's got the perfect excuse to get rid of me now."

"That's not fair, Jonathan," the Mouse reprimanded, pushing his glasses up higher on his nose for the tenth time. "If you wanted to stay with Louise, you just had to shape up. We've all given you plenty of chances. Now we're starting a new life in a new place and I expect you to get your act together."

Nicole was surprised at the Mouse's tone. She had never heard him sound stern before. "One big, happy family," she murmured, echoing Jonathan's words.

The waiter suddenly appeared and set a plate down in front of her. Nicole didn't remember ordering, but she was glad for the food. It gave her something to do, something to keep from looking at her mother and the Mouse. Eating would keep her from doing something very crazy, something that would embarrass her mother, something not very worthy of a Whitcomb.

In all her life Nicole had never felt more betrayed than she did right now. Her mother could at least have warned her. She could have said that she and Adam were serious about each other, and that he was different from her other boyfriends. At least she could have let on that Adam came complete with Jonathan.

It started to sink in—Adam as a stepfather, Jonathan as a stepbrother. The thought made her sicker than the queasy feeling she had had before. Suddenly, Nicole—of tea dances, of Miss Brill's charm classes, of the very best old-family Palm Beach manners, with never a hair out of place—wanted to jump up, overturn the table, and dump her chicken marsala all over the Mouse's bald head. Then she would run out of the Circle Dining Room screaming. She'd scream so loud that her father would hear her out there—wherever he was in the middle of the ocean—and turn his boat around and come and save her.

Instead, Nicole pushed her mushrooms from the right side of her plate to the left, and buried them beneath her rice.

Later that night, Nicole placed a ship-to-shore phone call.

"Dad?"

The voice on the other end was smothered with static. "Nicole, honey, is that you?" her father asked, yawning. "It's very late for you to be up, isn't it?"

"Yeah, Dad," she replied, curling her feet up under her long, striped sleep-shirt. With one hand she patted Neutron, her striped orange cat. "I know it's late, but . . ." she trailed off, suddenly not sure what to say. She was afraid that maybe her father had known her mother was marrying Adam Stanton, and hadn't told her.

"I know why you called," he broke in, suddenly serious, and Nicole held her breath. She was never really sure how much contact her mother had with her father. Their divorce had not been at all friendly, and her mother didn't like the fact that she had stayed close to her father. Still, Nicole knew they talked sometimes, about things that had to do with her. He must know that her mother was getting remarried.

"Wh—why?" Nicole stammered, trying not to sound scared.

"Because Christmas is next week, and I haven't let you know when I'm going to see you," Mr. Whitcomb replied.

Nicole frowned. With all these other worries tonight, she had almost forgotten about that. "No, you haven't," she admitted, chewing on a lock of hair.

"Now, don't be mad at me," he sounded like he felt bad about it. "But I can't make it this Christmas, hon."

"You what?" Nicole exclaimed, gasping. "But, Dad, we always see each other at Christmas, and . . ."

"And I hope this won't happen again, but . . ." Her father went on to explain that his expedition ship was about to start a major underwater experiment in the next three days. "We can't break off for Christmas," he concluded. "So I won't get to see you until the New Year."

Nicole nodded dumbly. "But, that's a few weeks from now."

"I know, and I'm sorry, hon," he apologized. "I'm really sorry to let you down."

"Oh, I understand," Nicole said, flatly. "I—I'm just going to miss you more than ever, this year."

"There's good news, though," he said, trying

to make her feel better. "I can stay in Palm Beach for almost three whole weeks."

"Once you get here."

"Right. . . ."

Nicole could picture how upset her father looked as he said that. She hurried to reassure him. It was bad enough that *she* felt terrible. "It's all right," she said again, trying to blink back her tears. She would not cry. "I do understand."

Her father's voice brightened at that. "I knew you would," he said, breathing a sigh of relief. "You're a daughter after my own heart. You understand how important my work is." Nicole really did understand. If she could, she wanted to be an explorer just like him.

They talked for a few more minutes, and then said goodnight.

Nicole slowly hung up the phone, not wanting to break contact with her father. Neutron climbed into Nicole's arms and began licking the salty streaks of her tears. "Oh, Neutron!" she wailed into the cat's thick orange fur. "This has to be the very worst night of my life." The orange tabby purred in agreement, as Nicole cried herself to sleep.

CHAPTER 3

The next afternoon, Esme was shuffling slowly across the stage of the Palm Beach Prep auditorium. She hunched her back, jutted out her chin, and tried to picture the ninety-eight-year-old woman she'd met at the Coconut Palm Rest Home last year when the glee club had performed there. When she saw the picture of the woman in her mind, she let her jaw go slack and tried to think old, very old.

With every slow step she took, her five white-blond braids bobbed up and down and the overstuffed pink Saks shopping bag she carried banged against her leg. A tape of Bing Crosby singing "I'm Dreaming of a White Christmas" played offstage. A group of girls, including Quinn, stood in the wings, making what Quinn's script described as "offstage party noises, clink of glasses, laughter, et cetera."

Esme approached the upholstered chintz sofa where Nicole was sitting straight and stiff as a stick. Even though it wasn't a dress rehearsal, Nicole was wearing her mustache, to get used to talking with it. But she had taped it on upside down. Esme stifled the impulse to laugh, forcing herself to think old, very old, very sick, very lonely bag lady about to be cast out into a terrible storm—a freak occurrence in Palm Beach.

Esme let out a cry that was definitely not in the script, and managed to squeeze out two real tears. She clasped her hands in front of her and staggered toward Nicole. "Sir, you won't send me out into that storm," Esme said in a quavery voice. "Not this night of all nights in the year. Not on Christmas." Esme fell to her knees and clutched the bottom of Nicole's green-and-blue-plaid uniform-skirt.

Nicole, who was playing the rich real-estate developer, Bart LeBarre, was supposed to jump up and step clear of Esme's outstretched hands. That was the way that they had rehearsed the scene all week. Instead, Nicole just sat there. She looked down at Esme and went blank. "Uh—ummm—"

Beside her on the sofa, Cara Knowles, who was playing the wife Lila LeBarre, let out an exasperated sigh. "Here we go again," she mumbled in disgust. She flipped her golden blond hair over her shoulder and narrowed her icy blue eyes at Nicole. From her vantage point in the wings, Quinn clenched and unclenched her fists. Cara could have at least whispered Nicole's line to help her out.

Quinn's gravelly voice carried right out to the audience as she prompted her friend. "Something about this woman . . . Lila, something about her reminds me of my own mother."

Nicole fidgeted slightly and tried to repeat the phrase. "My own mother . . . she's . . . uh . . . something like my own mother," she stammered, but it came out all jumbled. Nicole looked down at Esme and shrugged before saying, "Sorry. I can't seem to get anything straight today." She slumped back into the cushions of the sofa, even though her character in Quinn's play "Home for Christmas" wasn't the type to slouch at all.

"Caramba!" Alicia exclaimed from her first-row seat in the audience. With a jangle of earrings and big plastic bracelets, the dark, curly haired Cuban girl bounded up onto the stage. She planted her hands on her hips and faced Nicole. "Nicole," she scolded, and then paused. She hated to yell at one of her best friends, but she was the director, after all. "You're supposed to be upset that this terribly dirty person is touching you. Mr. LeBarre has never even looked at a

bag lady up close. No one really poor has ever been in his home before, have they?"

Nicole looked at the floor. She couldn't say anything that would make Alicia feel better, so she just kept quiet.

"Think of how *you* would feel if someone old and dirty walked right up to you and touched you," Alicia went on, trying to help Nicole.

Cara snickered. "She'd invite them in," she wheedled snidely, "like all the other strays she collects."

"Oh, shut up, Knowles-It-All!" Alicia ordered, whirling around. "Whatever's going on with Nicole doesn't concern you." Turning back to Nicole, Alicia waited a moment, giving her a chance to explain why she kept messing up today. "Nicole?" she finally asked.

Nicole slowly raised her head to look at Alicia. "Sorry, Lish," she apologized. "I forgot. I forgot what I was supposed to do, what to say. I guess memorizing lines is not my strong point." Nicole felt stupid defending herself. Her mind was just not on the play today, and that was perfectly obvious to herself and all her friends.

"The play is this Saturday afternoon, Nicole," Alicia admonished. "That's two days away, and you don't even know your lines." Alicia tossed her thick black curls, stomped over to the table, and plopped down in a chair.

"Her line, Alicia," Cara corrected nastily. "It's singular. Her line. Nicole only has one line."

"Two lines!" Esme almost yelled in Nicole's defense. "Nicole has two lines." She stood up and began adjusting the rubber band at the bottom of one of her braids.

Alicia squeezed her eyes shut. Quinn could see she was trying to control her temper. Alicia always seemed to speak first and think later. But this time, she really was trying to think first, and Quinn was impressed. Quinn also knew she had better do something quick, or Alicia might explode.

Alicia had been chosen over Cara to be director of the play by the faculty advisor Mr. Holmes and the entire sixth-grade drama group, except, of course, Cara's crowd. Cara, Jesse, Stephanie, Mimi, and Patty had made sure that life was not easy for Alicia. During every rehearsal they'd done their best to sabotage Alicia's efforts—nothing major—but enough to get on Alicia's nerves. Today, Patty had "accidentally" misplaced half the props. Yesterday, Cara had developed a very sudden and very short case of laryngitis. Last week, Stephanie had skipped rehearsal three days running. Her last excuse was a twisted ankle. Yet, she had been hanging out at Scoops after playing basketball with some of the G. Adams boys. And Jesse, who was stage manager, had put off painting the backdrop until today.

Quinn walked onstage, script in hand, pencil behind her ear. She blew her long red bangs off her forehead, took a steadying breath, and stopped in front of Nicole. "Something happened, didn't it?" she asked in a low voice, so no one else could hear.

"No," Nicole lied, and then added, "Nothing I can't handle anyway." She didn't like to lie to her friends. But her problems with her mother, the Mouse, and Jonathan, and her father were just too private to tell anyone about, even her best friends. Nicole squeezed her eyes shut. They felt all dried up, like her body did when she sat in the bathtub for too long. She knew it was from crying herself to sleep last night. Nicole vowed not to cry again because it made her feel disgusted with herself.

Cara watched them, gloating. She buffed her nails on the sleeve of her perfectly pressed navy-blue regulation blazer. Everything about her was perfectly pressed, right down to her socks. Cara held her perfectly manicured hands up to her face and admired them. "That's what Alicia gets for playing favorites," Cara murmured obnoxiously, just loud enough for Quinn and Nicole to hear. Cara flicked her long, smooth blond hair so that it fanned out behind her on the sofa. "Casting Nicole in anything but a walk-on role was a terrible mistake."

Jesse looked up from where she was painting the backdrop. "Well, the play is dumb," she said, waving her paintbrush at Cara. "You said so yourself."

Cara nodded. For the first time since she had come to Palm Beach Prep in first grade, she was not the star of the Christmas program. Cara would never let on that it upset her, not even to her best friend Jesse. But she would also never forgive that shrimp Alicia for choosing Esme to be the star instead of her. "I would never want to be the lead in this play," she added insultingly. "I mean, it's such a bad play! I definitely wouldn't want to associate myself with it so closely."

"It's true, Cara," Jesse agreed. "You wouldn't want to be a bag lady anyway. I saw the makeup and costume Esme has to wear. It's totally disgusting!"

"Cara's got a pretty good role, though," Mimi added shyly, from behind Jesse. Mimi had only come to Palm Beach Prep that fall, and she was the newest member of Cara's crowd. She had worked very hard to get Palm Beach Prep's sixth-grade social queen to become her friend. "It's better than Esme's by far. You get to wear a fur coat and pearls."

"That's right," Cara said, remembering why

she liked this role. She sat up straighter on the sofa, and looked brightly toward the door. Mrs. Hartman, the headmistress of the all-girls academy, was sailing into the room. Avery Holmes, the drama advisor, followed in her wake. Mrs. Hartman marched up the short flight of steps leading to the stage, and swept past Alicia, floating on a storm cloud of perfume. Mr. Holmes waited at the bottom of the stairs. All eyes turned in his direction—every girl in the school had a crush on him. Mrs. Hartman had to clear her throat twice to get everyone's attention away from Mr. Holmes.

"Good afternoon, girls," she said. Her commanding voice forced everyone's eyes to turn towards her.

"Good afternoon, Mrs. Hartman," all the girls chanted in unison.

"Mr. Holmes tells me that things are progressing quite nicely," Mrs. Hartman continued. She was having a little trouble accepting this play, even though Quinn's original story had been approved by the faculty for the Christmas program. The headmistress felt that the subject was unsuitable, not to mention unsavory. It was about a homeless woman who seeks shelter in a Palm Beach mansion during a terrible Christmas storm, and a long-lost runaway son who turns up at the door at midnight on Christmas Eve. This was not appropriate material for her sixth-grade girls, Mrs. Hartman thought. But what's done is done, and she only hoped that the play would at least go well. She didn't want any embarrassment for the school because of a shoddy performance.

"I have some rather wonderful news," Mrs. Hartman announced, getting to the point of her surprise visit to the rehearsal, "thanks to the generosity of Cara Knowles and her family." The headmistress pushed her glasses up on her very straight, long nose and smiled warmly at Cara.

"Caramba!" Alicia muttered. "What in the world is Knowles-It-All up to now?"

Quinn glanced in Cara's direction. She wore her usual smug expression, but looked a bit confused. "I don't think she knows," Quinn answered Alicia's question, surprising her. Alicia hadn't heard Quinn come up behind her. "I think Daddy Warbucks has something to do with this."

Esme giggled, having overheard Quinn. They all loved Quinn's latest nickname for Cara's millionaire father.

"First of all," Heartburn, the girls' pet nickname for Mrs. Hartman, continued. "Thanks to Mr. Knowles, we will have the services of Harry Blissmore, the makeup artist from the Royal Poinciana Playhouse, for the dress rehearsal tomorrow and the performance on Saturday."

The girls all looked at each other excitedly. A

real live makeup artist! Incredible! Cara positively glowed with pride.

"Es," Quinn pointed out, a bit too loudly. "He's going to make you look so old, you're going to look like your grandmother's grandmother."

"Miss McNair!" Mrs. Hartman reprimanded, her voice cutting through the girls' excitement. "May I continue?"

Quinn winced, but met Heartburn's eyes without flinching. She suspected that old Flo Hartman had a grudging respect for her, even though she would never admit it.

"Secondly, the entire cast is invited to a barbecue and party after the performance at the Knowles estate."

"What!?" Cara hissed, livid now. "I don't believe it. What does that idiot father of mine think he's doing? I don't *want* the entire cast at my house!" she grumbled, keeping her voice down so Heartburn couldn't hear. "I don't want the McNair crowd at my house ever, ever again."

When Quinn had first come to Palm Beach Prep that fall, she and Cara had gotten into a major fight. Cara had accused Quinn of stealing her watch, and Quinn had nearly been kicked out of school. The watch finally turned up—in Cara's own bag. It was the start of a long standing feud, between Cara and Company against Quinn and her three best friends.

"Do we have to go?" Quinn asked Nicole, for the third time.

"I think so, Quinn," Nicole answered, grateful to get the attention away from her mess-ups.

"You *are* the author, after all," Esme reminded Quinn.

"And I *am* the director," Alicia added, sorrowfully. "*Madre mia,* I thought that the election rally at Cara's was the absolute worst. I don't think I can make it through another one of her parties."

"Come on, guys," Esme urged. "It might be fun."

The other three rolled their eyes. Fun at the Knowles's estate was just not possible.

"Well, you never know," Esme insisted.

Alicia shrugged. "Ground yourself, Esme. I don't think that it'll be that much fun."

"Well," Quinn declared, with a toss of her red hair. "I don't know if I'll go. I don't care what Heartburn says."

CHAPTER 4

"Boycott. Boycott. Boycott," Quinn repeated over and over, as she, Esme, Nicole, and Alicia sat in Quinn's bedroom an hour later. She paused when she heard the microwave's bell ring, and then ran into the kitchen to get the freshly popped bag of popcorn. As she reentered the room, she continued. "We'll be making a statement if none of us go to the party."

Quinn plopped down on one of the floor cushions and stretched her long legs out in front of her. She had changed into her favorite pair of broken-in skinny black jeans. Nicole, Alicia, and Esme were still in their uniforms, but they'd shed their blazers. Quinn propped her feet on edge of the bed, and reached for the popcorn.

"I don't think so, Q," Alicia disagreed from in front of the wall mirror, where she was trying on Quinn's collection of weird earrings. Alicia hung a three-inch silver skeleton in her right ear, then frowned at her reflection. "I think we *should* go to Cara's. I mean, she doesn't want us there, and you know how I hate giving Cara what she wants."

Quinn chuckled suddenly. "You know, Lish," she said. "You just might have something there."

"What do you think, Nicole?" Esme asked, eying her.

Nicole was sitting cross-legged on Quinn's bed, watching the little battered black-and-white television on her nightstand. The evening news was on, and Nicole seemed to be engrossed in terrorist bombings, New York subway strikes, and lottery winners. She had a dazed look on her face, but the girls didn't think it was from the news. She didn't even turn at Esme's question. "Yeah, right," she responded, distractedly.

Alicia gave a disgusted snort. "Nicole, I hear Simon is going to have a baby," she said, testing Nicole's attention.

"Right," Nicole answered again.

"Two twins," Quinn added.

"Twin pigs," Esme put in, with a grin, thinking of Nicole's big bay stallion.

Nicole finally came out of her daze, "Huh?" she asked, confused. "What are you guys talking about?"

The other girls grinned at her. Nicole looked

sheepish. "Sorry," she murmured. "I wasn't paying attention. Who's having a baby?"

Quinn and Esme giggled, but Alicia looked a bit angry. "Nicole, we're talking about Cara's party and the Christmas play. The one you're in just two short days from now, remember?" she asked a little sarcastically.

"Just because I forgot my dumb lines doesn't mean I'll forget about the play," Nicole snapped back.

Quinn decided to step in and prevent a fight. She knew that Alicia was just nervous about directing, and Nicole was . . . well, she was upset about something. "Don't worry, Nicole," Quinn soothed. "You'll remember your lines tomorrow. Sometimes I think it's harder to have fewer lines. You sort of lose track of what's going on around you. Then you miss your cues."

Nicole finally smiled. It was the first smile her friends had seen all day. "I hadn't thought of that," she admitted. "Now I don't feel so bad."

"But we weren't really talking about the play, Nicole," Esme reminded. "We were wondering about Cara's party. Do you think we should go?"

Nicole shrugged. "Why not?" she asked, curiously. "We were invited, weren't we? Besides, Heartburn expects us to go."

"Nicole Whitcomb!" Quinn cried, outraged. Nicole tended to be a walking handbook of rules and regulations, at least as far as Palm Beach

Prep was concerned. Sometimes, she drove Quinn crazy, especially because Quinn felt very strongly that some rules were just made to be broken. "You can't always do things because other people expect you to. Sometimes, you have to take a stand."

Nicole had enough problems, and now Quinn was telling her that she had to change. "Listen, Quinn," she attacked, stung. "I don't always follow the rules, or do what people expect. I'm here, aren't I?"

Esme and Alicia stood up and applauded Nicole. "*Brava*, Nicole," Alicia congratulated her. "That's true, Quinn. Nicole's mother forbade her to come to Nueva Beach, and if she ever got caught she wouldn't be allowed to ride Simon for a whole month."

Quinn looked a little sheepish. "Yeah, I sort of forgot about that," she admitted. Then, she grinned at Nicole. "It's just that you *look* like you'd never do anything wrong."

Nicole looked down at her uniform, which was still as spotless, wrinkle-free, and as incredibly neat as it had been this morning. They did have a point. Sometimes she wished she could be a little more . . . well . . . like Quinn. "Looks," she said a little defensively, "can be deceiving."

"Beneath the cool, calm, collected Whitcomb exterior, is a wild rebel just dying to break out," Alicia teased, chuckling.

Nicole thought of Jonathan. He obviously looked down on her for being so "good," and for never breaking the rules. "Laugh all you want, Lish," she said. "I might surprise you someday."

"Speaking of surprises. . . ." Quinn reached up from the floor and turned the television volume higher. "What's the name of your father's boat again?"

"My dad's boat?" Nicole asked, turning away from Alicia. "The *Starry Night*," she said slowly. "Why?"

"I thought I heard something on the news," Quinn explained. "They said there was going to be a story about it after this commercial."

Nicole held her breath as everyone gathered around the television. What if something had happened to her father? Why would his boat be on television? Then, Sandra Sanchez, the newswoman, came back on the screen.

"Finally, tonight, the renowned undersea explorer, Captain Christopher Whitcomb—"

"It's him, it's him!" Esme shrieked. Two of Quinn's three brothers burst into the room, attracted by Esme's screaming.

"What's going on?" Sean cried, pushing his longish auburn hair out of his eyes.

"Shhh!" Alicia hissed, not even looking at the sixteen-year-old. "It's Nicole's father. Something's happened to his boat." She patted Nicole's shoulder. "*Carina,* I'm sure he's okay."

Nicole couldn't reply. She couldn't even look at anyone else. Photos of her father and his ship were taking up the entire screen. What if something had happened to her father? What would she do then?

Finally, Sandra Sanchez got to the point of her story. "Captain Whitcomb's ship, the *Starry Night,* is experiencing some minor engine trouble after a small shipboard fire, and must put to dock in Key West this weekend for repairs. According to the Coast Guard, captain and crew are fine. The *Starry Night* is traveling under its own power, at half-speed toward port, accompanied by a Coast Guard vessel. It is due to arrive in Key West sometime late Saturday or Sunday."

"Oh, thank goodness he's okay," Nicole said, relieved. She sagged back against Alicia, then turned around, her eyes shining. "I'm so glad everything's all right."

"So that's your father?" Sean asked, impressed.

"Isn't it wild!" Esme exclaimed.

Nicole just sat in front of the television, grinning. Her father was all right. He was putting in at Key West this weekend. His boat was okay. She heard the anchorwoman conclude, ". . . interfere much with the purpose of this expedition. The *Starry Night* will be docked in Key West for only one to two days."

Two days. Her dad would be in Key West for two whole days. This weekend. Suddenly, she sat bolt upright. Two days, this weekend, in Key West. Key West wasn't very far from Palm Beach. There had to be a bus that went there. A plane would be just too expensive. Nicole knew there was a Greyhound station near Esme's house in West Palm Beach.

"Bus. . . ." she murmured aloud.

"What?" Esme asked sharply, looking at her. Why was Nicole suddenly looking better than she had all day?

"Oh, nothing," Nicole said, then looked at her watch. If she really was going to go down to Key West to see her father, she had a lot of planning to do. There'd be a million things to think about—how to keep her grandparents from finding out, how to get to the bus station, where to leave her bike, when exactly she should leave, and stuff like that.

"Hey, guys," she interrupted everyone. "I've got to go." She jumped up and grabbed her blazer.

"Wait, my mom's going to order pizza," Quinn reminded. "We were counting on you to help us eat it."

"Some other time," Nicole yelled as she ran out of the room. "I just remembered there's something very important I have to do."

CHAPTER 5

On Saturday morning, Nicole took extra time making her bed. She smoothed every wrinkle out of the pale blue spread. She carefully hung up her long white-and-yellow terry robe, and then tucked her slippers into the shoe bag on her closet door.

When she was finished, she took one last look around her room. The sun was streaming through the window, dancing across her collection of blue ribbons which hung on the wall above her trophy shelf. Her school books were stacked neatly on her huge, polished oak desk. *Black Stallion*, *Misty*, and *Fury* books filled Nicole's shelves. Her collection of glass, metal, marble, and plastic horse-figurines took up the entire space in front of the books on the shelves. She bit her lip as she picked up the tiniest brass horse. Esme had given it to her when she was only six, because, even then, Nicole had been crazy about horses. She shoved it into the front pocket of her jeans and grabbed her yellow sweatshirt before looking around one last time. She loved her room—she was really going to miss it.

Before she left, Nicole gave Neutron one last pat. The tabby purred in his sleep and stretched a paw toward her hand. Then, he curled up into an orange ball in the sweater drawer Nicole always left open for him. Nicole hoped that her grandmother would take care of the stray cat that she had adopted three months before. Without looking back, she left the room and tiptoed down the back stairs.

Once in the kitchen, she stuffed a couple of oranges, a package of Oreos, and a bagful of her grandmother's homemade Christmas cookies into her knapsack. She carefully propped the note to her grandparents against the coffee maker on the counter. She started toward the door, and then went back to check her note one last time. She wanted to be absolutely sure that it was believable:

> Didn't want to wake you so early. Am off to Esme's to rehearse for the play this afternoon. I will spend tonight and tomorrow

night at her house. Sorry you can't make the performance.

Nicole stopped to consider that last sentence. Disaster would certainly strike if her grandmother suddenly felt guilty about missing the play and showed up this afternoon. Still, Nicole was pretty sure that the caterers were coming over to discuss the wedding, and her grandparents would be busy talking to them.

I'll miss you there. If mom calls from New York later, give her my love. I love you. Nicole.
P.S. Don't forget to feed Neutron.

Nicole put the note back on the counter and walked out of the house. It was only when she opened the garage to get her bike that she realized that she had been holding her breath for the last thirty seconds.

"Calm down," she scolded herself. She inhaled deeply ten times, letting her breath out slowly, pretending that she was on her way to compete in a horse show. "Nerves," she reminded herself, "are not bad." They actually help you do better. Candy Gordon, her riding instructor at PBP, was always telling her that.

Wheeling her bike from the garage, she glanced up. It was cool, but the sky was already ultra blue, with a few puffy white clouds sailing above her. It was a perfect day for riding—or setting off on an adventure. "It's going to be a great day," she told herself, as she tied the blue-and-yellow-silk "I love LaLa land" scarf in her hair. Esme had been to Hollywood for a screen test and had given it to her as a gag gift when she got back. It was really pretty tacky, but Nicole loved it.

Reaching the end of her driveway, Nicole adjusted the straps of her knapsack, hopped on her bike, and pedaled off. She rode quickly through the streets, deserted at this early hour on a Saturday morning. She slowed only when she passed the gates to PBP. It took every ounce of willpower she had not to stop off to see Simon. Nicole planned to call Quinn and ask her to take care of him and bring him carrots and sugar, but not until next week. She didn't really have time to stop anyway, according to what the guy at the Greyhound station had said when she called. The first bus left for Key West really soon. Key West—and her father, her final destination, were both in sight.

Thinking of her father, Nicole pedaled faster and was soon downtown. The Christmas lights on all the trees were off, but the wreaths and holly bounced up and down in the slight breeze. Nicole suddenly hesitated. She had never spent a Christmas away from home before.

But even as she realized it, she reminded herself that she *would* be home for Christmas—home with her father on the *Starry Night*. Nicole hadn't given it any more thought apart from the fact that she was moving in with her father—out of her mother's house. Lots of divorced kids changed the parents they lived with. She knew that lawyers would have to get involved at some point or something like that. But she wasn't going to worry about it. Her parents could deal with all that. And now her mother would have Adam and Jonathan to worry about, so she didn't really need Nicole. Jonathan was all the causes her mother had ever worked for in one person.

Luckily, no one would think she was missing for a few days. Her mother was in New York until at least tomorrow night, and her note had taken care of the rest of the family.

Nicole pedaled to a stop a few doors down from Esme's, got off her bike, and walked it the rest of the way. She guided her ten-speed across Esme's small lawn and through the open wooden gate that led to the back of the Farrell's garage. She put the bike behind a cluster of azaleas, making sure it was entirely hidden.

Nicole practically jumped out of her Reeboks when the next-door-neighbor's dog suddenly started barking. All she needed was for Esme to hear the dog and wake up. She bolted out of the bushes, cut across some yards, and finally got to the street behind Esme's house. She ran as fast as she could. Then it dawned on her that someone might wonder what an eleven-year-old girl was doing running full speed down the deserted streets of West Palm Beach so early on a Saturday morning. She forced herself to slow down to a jog, reaching the station at First Street just as the Greyhound bus marked "Key West" pulled in.

Inside, the station was almost deserted. Only one old woman was in front of her in the ticket line. Nicole looked straight ahead and nervously kept shifting her weight from one foot to the other. She half-expected someone to tap her on the shoulder and ask what she was doing there alone, at eight-thirty on a Saturday morning. But she resisted the impulse to keep turning around. And the woman ahead of her was so slow. She acted as if she was moving through water. Nicole didn't think she would ever get her wallet zipped, at the rate she was going. Nicole reached back to finger her scarf for reassurance. She gasped. *It was gone!* The old woman turned around at Nicole's exclamation.

"Lost something?" she asked.

Nicole gulped. She didn't like talking to people, especially strangers. "Just a scarf," she mumbled.

"Well, let's look around for it," the woman offered.

"Uh—I don't have time," Nicole sputtered. "I don't want to miss my bus," she explained, stepping quickly up to the counter. "One way to Key West, please," she asked the ticket man, rubbing her very sweaty palms on her thighs. She was sure the man would be able to tell she was running away and that he would try and stop her.

"That'll be thirty-four dollars."

Nicole undid the Velcro flap on her wallet. She counted out a twenty, a ten, and four ones. She tried not to look at the two ten-dollar bills left. It was all the money she had until she found her father.

"Change buses in Miami," the clerk instructed her. "Key West is the last stop." For some reason, he started laughing. "Nowhere to go from there," he added, ambling over to the coffee machine. Nicole just stood there, staring at him for a moment. He made it sound as if she was going to get on the bus and vanish right off the edge of the world or something.

Suddenly, Nicole felt like going home. She hadn't known she would have to change buses in Miami, or anything like that. Maybe taking a bus alone to see her father wasn't such a good idea. It was the sort of thing Jonathan would do, or maybe Quinn. But it wasn't something Nicole Whitcomb would do.

The old woman walked up to Nicole. "I looked

in the ladies' room, girl, and it wasn't there," she rasped.

"What wasn't there?" Nicole asked, confused, finally moving away from the ticket window.

"Your scarf," the woman said. "Now, what color was it?"

"Oh," Nicole mumbled. "It doesn't matter."

The P.A. system crackled to life. "Next bus for Key West boarding at Gate Two," the ticket-master's voice announced through a burst of static.

"Don't know why he goes through all that," the woman grumbled, as she slowly made her way toward the gate. "Could have told us what gate and all that when we bought our tickets."

Nicole shouldered her knapsack and followed the woman. She didn't want to stand around the waiting room any longer than she had to. Some-one who knew her might turn up. But then she thought that no one would even miss her. She could be gone a whole week and her mother probably wouldn't even notice.

The driver was standing outside his bus, smok-ing a cigarette and sipping coffee from a Dunkin' Donuts cup. The bus door was still closed, even though it was already eight-thirty. Nicole glanced over her shoulder a little nervously. She was still worried that someone she knew would show up at the bus station.

"When can we get on?" she asked the driver in a soft voice.

"The bus won't leave until eight forty-five," the driver answered, and went back to his coffee. He didn't seem to be in any hurry. By the time he emptied his mug and snuffed out his cigarette, the line behind Nicole was joined by three men and a woman with two young children.

"Traveling alone?" the older woman asked Nicole, startling her.

"Uh—yes," Nicole answered, feeling her cheeks grow hot. *Did this woman know that she was running away? How?* "My father is down in Key West and I'm going to visit him for Christmas," she explained, as she stepped up onto the bus.

"You'll have to change buses in Miami, then," the woman said. She had obviously made this trip before. "I'm switching there, too. Now, it's best to sit in the front seat, here," she offered, gesturing to the seat right behind the driver. "That way, no one bothers you, a pretty girl traveling alone." The woman let Nicole have the window seat, and then sat down next to her.

Nicole hadn't thought of that. She hadn't stopped to think how dangerous it could be to be young and alone until then. "Thanks," she murmured, and gratefully leaned back in the seat. A few minutes later, as the bus pulled out of the station, Nicole wondered if there was anything else she had forgotten about. All the terrible stories about runaways flashed before her eyes. She shuddered.

"Are you okay, girl?" the old woman asked her.

Nicole looked up, startled. "I'm fine," she murmured softly. "I was just thinking."

"Buses are good for that, for thinking about things," the woman agreed. "Now, I've traveled some twenty thousand miles around this country on buses. I wouldn't travel any other way. Good time for getting your thoughts straight." She paused, and then looked at Nicole thoughtfully. "Though at your age I would say there shouldn't be quite that much to think about." The woman went on about her very first bus trip alone when she was only seventeen and on her way to visit her husband-to-be who was in the army in San Francisco.

Nicole half-listened. Thank goodness the woman didn't know just how much she had to think about. Nicole closed her eyes and tried to imagine how her father would react to her sudden appearance. She wasn't sure what she was going to say to him, only that she wanted to live with him from now on. She could take correspondence courses while the *Starry Night* sailed around the world. She had read about some kids who did that. Nicole was a straight-A student now, and school was a breeze.

She would miss her friends, though. Nicole frowned, hoping Quinn and Alicia would understand about their play. Her acting had been so bad lately that she was sure they would be glad to have an understudy take over for her. Nicole couldn't remember who her understudy was, but whoever she was, she had to be better than Nicole had been. Quinn and Alicia would get over her skipping out of their play, especially after she had a chance to explain why she had to miss it.

Nicole fidgeted in her seat. It was a long trip to Key West, and already it felt like she couldn't sit still a moment longer. She propped her feet up on the railing in front of her, and clasped her arms around her knees.

Nicole wished, not for the first time, that she didn't find it so hard to talk to her friends. She gazed wistfully out the window, as flashes of water, blue sky, and puffy white clouds whizzed by. If only she could be as outgoing as Alicia, as outspoken as Quinn, or as self-centered as Esme. Then she would think that everyone else in the world was interested in the gory details of her life.

Alicia had teased her just the other day for keeping so many secrets. Remembering the moment, Nicole looked at her hands, and then stared back out at the passing scenery. She didn't mean to keep secrets. It was just that some things hurt too much to talk about.

She tried to imagine day after day on the *Starry Night* without Alicia, Quinn, and, especially, Esme. She suddenly felt kind of empty inside. She turned her thoughts to her father and felt much better. Long before they reached Miami, Nicole drifted off to sleep, dreaming of the *Starry Night* and how great it would be to sail around the world.

For the past few months, Esme had devoted every Saturday morning to her beauty routine. She started out with a facial, complete with mud pack, then she gave herself a manicure, pedicure, and rubbed her calluses away with pumice. Finally she would take a long, hot soak in the tub, while deep-conditioning her hair. Turning on WPLM to listen to the Top 40 countdown, she would usually hear the entire forty songs before her treatment was finished. At the age of twelve, she really didn't need to go through this every week, but having the ambition to be famous was quite a burden. Esme felt as if she had to put herself through this routine to ensure her success.

Esme had just finished filling the tub when the phone rang. She reached under the bed and finally unearthed it from a pile of lost socks and several large dust bunnies. They could easily have been called dust elephants, or dust dogs.

"Hello!" she shouted over her radio's blare. "Quinn, is that you?"

A voice answered her, very faintly. "Just a sec!" she screamed again, and wriggled out from under the bed. She was covered with dust. She turned off the radio, and was a little surprised at how deathly quiet her room seemed. She stepped over the piles of clothes, organized into clean and dirty, and flopped down in her chair to settle in for a long talk.

"Quinn?" she asked again.

But, it wasn't Quinn. It was Sonia Hanson, Esme's modeling agent.

"Hi, sweetie," Sonia greeted her. "I hope you've got your bags packed."

"What bags?" Esme asked, confused, looking at the pink Saks bag that she was going to use for this afternoon's play. She had a pile of stuff to put in it—torn panty hose, a red flannel nightgown her father had gotten her when he took her skiing once, a torn uniform-blouse, and a battered pair of old-lady lace-up boots that she had found at the Salvation Army store in Nueva Beach.

"The booking came through, love," Sonia informed her, patiently.

"You mean for *Sassy*?" Esme asked excitedly. "In Key West?" Esme let out a loud whoop.

"The other blond model who was supposed to be working this weekend had to cancel—flu or something, and so they need you to come down there and fill in."

Esme suddenly felt deflated. "You mean *this* weekend, like, today?" she asked, not really wanting to know.

"You got it!" Sonia exclaimed. "So can you be ready in, say, forty-five minutes? I've got a car coming out to pick you up. We'll have you down there this afternoon."

"Uh," Esme began and then hesitated. Leaving meant missing the play. Esme and Nicole had been in every Christmas play together since kindergarten. Nicole was going to be pretty mad at her for this, but then again, Nicole had been acting strange all week. She always got a little weird at Christmas. Esme guessed it was because of her parents' divorce, which had been much worse than Esme's own parents' divorce—at least her mother and father still talked to each other. But this week she was acting even weirder than usual. Esme knew that sooner or later she'd have to pry Nicole's problem out of her.

Sonia's voice brought her back to the present situation. "Meanwhile, I had better talk to your mother about chaperons and such. I know she's going to be up in Tampa Bay for some business."

"Sure, let me get her for you," she answered, putting the phone down and yelling for her mother. Then, she ran back into the bathroom to have her bath while her mother straightened out all the details. She knew her mother would say yes. Lucy Farrell took Esme's modeling career very seriously.

Half an hour later, Esme and her mother were packing. "Now don't forget," Esme reminded her mother for the umpteenth time, "to call Quinn or Alicia and tell them that I have to miss the play. They are going to *kill* me!"

"Don't be ridiculous, dear," her mother answered, walking her out to the waiting car, and kissing her good-bye. "Your friends know that your career comes first."

"But it's the Christmas play, and I was the star, and now . . ." Esme felt terrible, then suddenly a thought struck her and things brightened considerably. "Cara Knowles will have to be a bag lady," she said under her breath, as she remembered who her understudy was. The thought of vain Cara in a role she couldn't stand, wearing saggy, torn stockings, polyester clothes, and a stringy gray wig, in front of most of Palm Beach's snobby society people lessened Esme's depression as she sank into the backseat of the limo. Her good mood lasted all the way to the airport.

CHAPTER 6

"Watching the sunset is a ritual here in Key West," the bus driver told Nicole as they crossed the final stretch of bridge on the Overseas Highway and approached the last of the chain of islands known as the Florida Keys. "Everybody does it."

"You mean, like tourists," Nicole replied, as she shook her silky hair back from her face and fished in her knapsack for her barrettes. She had done and undone her hair three times since leaving Miami. She wanted to make sure she looked just right when she saw her dad. She felt pretty gross from spending six hours sitting on a bus. Nicole couldn't wait to walk around. She'd never sat still for so long in her entire life.

"Sure, y'all get your tourists, especially at this time of year. But *everyone* goes to the pier—year-round residents and people just docked for the day or evening. It's a regular circus." The driver chuckled, and proceeded to describe the street performers, jugglers, and musicians who gathered to entertain the crowd while they waited for the sun to go down.

Nicole leaned forward eagerly in her seat. She gave her low ponytail a final tug, and then turned to look out the window. She couldn't believe how big Key West seemed. She thought it would be a small town, but it was definitely much more like a city. The houses were crowded close together. Tall, white apartment buildings mushroomed along either side of the road. "Is the pier far from the depot?" Nicole asked, wondering if they'd make it through the heavy traffic down to the bus terminal at Duvall Street before the sun set.

"Not far at all," the driver said easily. "Might even get you there before the sun goes down."

For the first time all day, Nicole smiled. The pier was the perfect place to go. If the *Starry Night* was in port, then there was a good chance her father would be there. If he wasn't, at least it gave her a place to go until she either found her father or figured out where she was going to spend the night.

She hopped off the bus as soon as it pulled into the station. A few minutes later she was still standing outside the terminal, feeling lost. She looked first to her right, then to her left. The bus driver's directions to the pier had sounded clear enough, but when Nicole looked around, all she saw were parking lots. Right across the street was a club. Even though it was only five-thirty, music with a strong Latin beat boomed out of the open doors. The strong, spicy smell of refried beans and chili filled the air. Overhead, the sky was already a blaze of brilliant colors. It reminded Nicole of Alicia's room, where purple clashed with orange and red. Nicole squashed the thought. Thinking of her friends right now was a bad idea. Her life in Palm Beach was behind her. She had more than enough to think about, wondering how she'd find her father. And what she would do with herself tonight if she couldn't.

She looked at the scrap of paper in her hand. The bus driver had quickly sketched her a map. She was supposed to find a place called Mallory Square. The pier was right near there.

"Hey, little girl, where are you going?"

Nicole's head snapped up. She looked right into the beady eyes of a fat man in khaki pants, a short-sleeved shirt, and a broad-brimmed khaki hat. He looked her up and down, and frowned. Nicole gulped. Then she noticed the metal badge pinned to his left shirt pocket. It was in the shape of a star and it said "Sheriff." He was also wearing a small black name tag—M. Trebaye.

Nicole's knees felt as if they were going to buckle underneath her. "Where am I going?" she finally gasped in a very small voice. The sheriff's beady eyes got even smaller.

"A girl your age . . ." he let the sentence trail off as he pulled out a very official looking little black book. "The bus driver warned me about a runaway and I—"

Nicole frantically tried to think of something to say. Then she remembered her mother, Adam, and Jonathan. "I'm no runaway," she replied with a dignity that surprised even her.

The sheriff stopped writing in his book. "You came here alone, didn't you?"

Nicole swallowed hard. "Yes, I did, Sheriff Trebaye." Nicole prayed she'd pronounced his name correctly. It must have been okay because he smiled a little and rocked back on his heels. Suddenly, he didn't seem like such a frightening person. She toyed with the idea of telling him the truth, or at least part of the truth. She could tell him that she was here to meet her father. If she mentioned her dad's name, he'd take her right to him. Nicole was almost sure of that—except . . . Nicole bit her lip. Except that her father had no idea she was coming in the first place. If the sheriff tried to reach him and he wasn't docked yet, or, if he called her mother . . . No, she couldn't risk it.

Just then, Nicole heard some girls giggling.

She turned to see three girls walking by wearing white shorts and carrying ice cream cones. One of them had a copy of *Sassy* magazine. Suddenly, Nicole remembered how Esme had told them all about the *Sassy* shoot she'd been so anxious about—it was here in Key West. Esme's job didn't start until next week. But the shoot was already in progress. Nicole smiled.

"You see, Sheriff," Nicole said in her most prissy Palm Beach Prep voice, "I'm here for the *Sassy* shoot." She paused for just an instant, trying to look very modest. "I'm a model." Then, conscious of how thin and flat-chested she was, she added quickly. "For young teen-fashion, you know." Nicole felt a little sick after she'd said that. In her entire eleven and a half years, she had told almost no lies—not even teeny weeny white lies—and now she was lying like a pro.

The sheriff's tight-lipped smiled stretched into a nice broad grin. "I should have guessed. Sorry, miss," he chuckled, as he hooked his thumbs in his belt loops. "I hope you don't mind me saying this. You sure are pretty enough to be a model, but you look a little young. And we keep a sharp eye out here at the depot for runaways. This is a nice town, but it's not a good place for a young girl alone." He shoved his hat further back on his round, balding head and scratched his forehead. Nicole felt as if she could almost see the wheels turning in his mind. "I thought that all the models had already arrived by plane earlier this afternoon."

Remembering Esme, Nicole was quick to reply. "Most of them did, but I got a last minute call . . . I . . . was at Key Largo with my family for the holidays, and then my agent called, so I caught the bus." Nicole couldn't get over how well she was lying. Then, her heart stopped. What if the bus driver had told the sheriff that he'd picked her up in Miami with a ticket that originated in Palm Beach?

Sheriff Trebaye was still grinning, though. He stuck out his pudgy hand and introduced himself, "Melvin Trebaye here. And you're—"

"Esme Farrell!" Nicole couldn't believe herself, but Esme's name was the first that had come to her mind. At least if the sheriff checked up on her, he'd find out that Esme really was a model. Nicole suddenly remembered something. "You see, I was supposed to start shooting next week, but there was this emergency and I—"

The sheriff's beeper sounded. He looked down and checked it. "Got to call in, but if you need anything while you're here, Miss Farrell, you just let Melvin Trebaye know and I'll help you."

He walked off, but then turned around quickly and gave Nicole a sheepish look. "Golly, miss, do you know the way to your hotel? I'm sorry, I forgot to ask."

Nicole had to think quickly, since she didn't

have the foggiest idea what the name of the hotel was. "The thing is that I've never been to Key West before and I don't know anything about it except where Mallory Square is, thanks to the bus driver."

"Oh, the Coral Grove." He nodded approvingly. Apparently, though it seemed like a city, Key West was more like a small town. Nicole figured the *Sassy* shoot must be big news if everyone knew where the models were staying.

"It's a very nice place. I wouldn't mind my own daughters staying there—chaperoned, of course," he added quickly. "You can walk. It's only a few blocks, down Duvall and then make a left."

Nicole thanked him and walked down Duvall. The main street was thronged with people coming back from the pier. The sun had just set. Nicole knew she'd have to be patient since she'd missed this chance to find her dad. She tried to ignore the rumbling in her stomach as she passed a row of sidewalk cafes. She was afraid to spend the little money she had, and decided to splurge on a candy bar later. Nicole wondered where the repair docks were, and if she should look for her dad's boat there—except that it was dark out and repair crews probably didn't work on Saturday night. Then she worried about the sheriff still being around and whether he'd notice if she didn't go right to the hotel.

She slowed down her pace and pretended to gaze into the window of a chic clothing store. Carefully, she looked over her shoulder, trying to seem as casual as possible. As she suspected, the sheriff was still in sight. He was in a phone booth on the corner. As soon as he noticed her staring in his direction, he waved. She waved back. That settled it. Nicole decided checking out the Coral Grove was the only sensible thing to do. She had no idea whether Sheriff Trebaye had believed her story. Nicole didn't want to take a chance.

The Coral Grove really was beautiful. It was a large, white Victorian-style building fringed with palm trees and bordered by a zillion flowery shrubs. As soon as Nicole walked into the lobby, a bellhop appeared. "Evening, miss. You must be with the *Sassy* people." He looked down at her hands and then glanced behind her back. "Your . . . er . . . luggage. . . ." he stammered, looking astonished that she didn't seem to have any.

Nicole shook her head. "My bags . . . uh . . . they got lost on the flight down here. Somewhere between—" she remembered in the nick of time not to say Palm Beach—"Washington and Miami!" she concluded a bit shrilly.

The bellhop nodded sympathetically. "What a drag!" He smiled. "Well, you can check in over there. The other models have been coming and going all day. I guess you weren't on the shoot this afternoon, though."

Nicole almost said she had been, but then realized that she wasn't even wearing makeup. Actually, she wasn't sure whether she'd be wearing makeup after a shoot or not. But just in case she answered, "No, I just got in. I . . . I . . . uh . . . don't work until tomorrow." She crossed her fingers, hoping that the models were working tomorrow even though it was Sunday.

"That's the big day, from what I hear. The main desk is that way," the bellhop continued cheerfully. "And by the way, my name is Mickey if you need me." He bounced off, and Nicole stood rooted to the spot.

"Miss, you check in here!" the man behind the main desk called from across the almost empty lobby. "You're with the *Sassy* people?" He started flipping through a clipboard.

"Let's see," he mumbled. "Which one are you?" he looked down and muttered several names out loud. "Andrea, Jasmine, Moira, Esme—"

"Esme!" Nicole said immediately, totally surprised to hear her friend's name.

"Esme Farrell," the man nodded, and started to write in some book. Nicole stared at the man. He thought she was Esme. That might actually work. Nicole walked right up to the front of the desk. She would sign in as Esme. Obviously, whoever was in charge of the shoot had booked rooms for *all* the models, whether they were starting this week or next. Nicole could pretend she was Esme. Then she wouldn't have to worry about getting a room. What harm could that do? It was for just one night.

"Sign right here," the desk clerk said brusquely, shoving the book in her direction, as he turned his back to answer the phone.

Nicole picked up a pen. Suddenly, she heard a breathy and unmistakable giggle floating in from the hotel entrance. Nicole froze. "Esme!" she breathed, and whirled around. Through a stand of potted palms, she spotted a mop of white-blond curls. *How could Esme be here?* Right this moment she was supposed to be back home in Palm Beach taking curtain calls at the end of Quinn's play. Of course, Nicole knew that she was supposed to be there too, but still. Nicole couldn't believe her eyes. By some incredible stroke of bad luck, Esme was here. Nicole dropped the pen, and bolted around the corner. She pressed herself close against the wall between a vending machine and a bank of phone booths.

"May I help you?" Nicole heard the desk clerk ask. Cautiously, she poked her head around the corner. She could see Esme standing there, surrounded by what looked like all the luggage she owned—two suitcases, a duffle bag, a makeup case, and a knapsack. No wonder the bellhop had been surprised when Nicole had turned up empty-handed. Apparently, models didn't travel light.

Nicole couldn't get over the way Esme looked. She had on tons of makeup, so she must have just been on a shoot. That meant she must have been in Key West for a little while, at least. Nicole was confused.

Esme turned to the woman who was standing next to her who looked to be in her early twenties. "Am I supposed to sign in?" she asked.

"Yes," the woman replied as she turned to the desk clerk. "I'm Sarah Wood. I'm the chaperon with the *Sassy* group—"

"And the makeup artist!" Esme informed the clerk with a toss of her blond curls.

He returned Esme's smile. "And you're?"

"Esme. Esme Farrell!"

The desk clerk pushed his glasses up higher on his nose and frowned at Esme. Nicole cringed. "Didn't you have brown hair a minute ago?" the clerk continued, his frown deepening.

Esme stared at him with big blue eyes. Then she began to giggle. "You think *this* is a wig?!" She giggled again and tugged on her hair. "See, it's real. I'm a natural blond!"

Nicole had to smile. Esme was such a ham. The desk clerk started to laugh, and Nicole let out a relieved sigh.

"I don't think any more models are due until tomorrow morning at the earliest," Sarah told the clerk. Nicole's ears perked up. "Jasmine Bartlett won't be here until tomorrow night, for sure. But do hold her room. She's on a booking now in L.A., but if her job ends sooner, she'll be flying right here. I don't want to lose her room."

"Jasmine Bartlett," Nicole murmured to herself. She ducked back into the phone booth just as Esme, Sarah, and the bellhop rounded the corner. Nicole remembered that she had actually met Jasmine once after one of Esme's shoots at the Poinciana Shopping Plaza. So what if Jasmine had bright-red curls. She wasn't turning up for at least twenty-four hours, which meant that Nicole had a place to stay tonight. If only she could convince the desk clerk that she was really Jasmine Bartlett after her first attempt at telling him that she was Esme Farrell.

Nicole approached the desk timidly. She took a deep breath. "Uh . . . I was checking in before and suddenly had to make a call," she murmured in what she hoped sounded like a Southern drawl. Jasmine was from Alabama, and was already pretty famous. Nicole worried that he might know who she was, since she was already a cover girl. She prayed that he wouldn't connect the name with the trademark red curls.

The clerk peered intently at Nicole. "Now, what did you say your name was?"

Nicole blushed slightly. "I . . . I . . . didn't. I'm not even supposed to be here yet, except that they rescheduled my last shoot in L.A."

"Oh, you must be Jasmine," the clerk said with a smile. "Jasmine Bartlett. Miss Wood, your chaperon, mentioned that there was an outside chance you'd be here tonight." He pushed the book in Nicole's direction so she could sign in.

"You've got one of the private rooms, Number 409. It's a beaut with a good ocean view. You'll like it." He handed her a room key, and she headed toward the stairs. "Just so you know," the clerk called after her, "the other models are meeting down at Mallory Square to go to dinner."

"Oh, thanks," Nicole replied quickly as she made a mental note to stay as far away from Mallory Square as possible. With a quick glance toward the desk, she ducked out a side door and hurried down the street in the direction of the water. Nicole was sure that someone down by the docks would know if the *Starry Night* had come in. She had no time to lose. If she didn't find her dad, she could at least go back to the Coral Grove tonight. Meanwhile, she had to avoid running into Esme at all costs—at least until she found her father.

CHAPTER 7

Cara Knowles sailed in front of the red-brocade curtain and curtsied. In spite of Esme's sudden cancellation and Nicole's mysterious disappearance, Quinn's play "Home for Christmas" had gone off without a hitch. It had actually been a huge success.

Cara kept her head bowed low for an instant, cursing the ugly print of the rayon bag-lady costume she had on. To think that her moment of glory was marred by having to wear such a tacky dress.

The Palm Beach Prep auditorium thundered with applause. Cara looked up from beneath her stringy gray wig and raised her tear-filled pale blue eyes toward the audience. Then, slowly, she rose up to her full height with her head thrown back, soaking in the applause.

"Cara, get back here!" Avery Holmes commanded from behind the curtain.

Cara didn't budge, and instead began to smile broadly. With a dramatic flourish, she raised her hand to her head and whipped off her wig. Her mane of silky dark-blond hair tumbled down around her shoulders. The audience cheered even more loudly, as Cara marched proudly off the stage. "That'll show them I'm no bag lady," she grumbled, as she elbowed her way past Quinn.

"That took you long enough," Quinn hissed at Cara. She straightened the jacket of her costume. Filling in for Nicole had been one of the worst experiences of Quinn's life. She loved writing plays, but she hated acting in them, even when she only had to say two lines. At least she had managed to pull it off, and the rest of the cast had been great. Quinn grabbed Stephanie Barnes's hand. Stephanie reached for Anne Marie Hayes, who giggled and grabbed Virginia Choy. The four girls slipped in front of the curtain and took their bows.

"A wonderful job, Cara!" Mrs. Hartman beamed, as the foursome squeezed by to allow the last three members of the cast to take their bows. "You did remarkably well, considering the circumstances."

"Thank you, Mrs. Hartman," Cara murmured as she lowered her gaze and blushed prettily underneath her thick bag-lady makeup. "With more rehearsing, and if it had been my part to start with, I would have been even better."

Mrs. Hartman frowned. "Esme Farrell may be talented, but she's not reliable. And as for Nicole Whitcomb—"

"I'm sure there's a perfectly good explanation for why Nicole's not here, Mrs. Hartman," Mr. Holmes said. "Alicia is trying to call her house again now. Some emergency must have come up. When she tried before the play, she only got the answering machine."

Quinn didn't stick around backstage long enough to hear any more. She slipped through the wings and, still in costume, went down the short flight of stairs that led into the hall. Alicia's dark curly head was bent low over the phone. She looked up when she heard Quinn coming. Her round face was screwed up with worry. She cupped her hand over the receiver. "No one's answered yet, not even the machine—" She broke off quickly. "Mrs. Todd?" Alicia sank back against the wall with relief. "Uh . . . I was wondering . . . do you know where Nicole is?"

Quinn leaned forward, and Alicia tilted the receiver so she could hear.

Mrs. Todd answered, "Oh, yes. Nicole left me a note. She's spending the weekend with Esme."

"With *Esme*?!" Alicia shrieked, then winced to hear how loud her voice sounded in the empty corridor. "She's with Esme!" Alicia mouthed to Quinn, her dark eyes flashing. *"Caramba!"* she shouted as she hung up and threw her hands in the air. She glared at Quinn and then kicked the wall. "Ooowww!" she howled, and began hopping on one sandaled foot.

Quinn started laughing. "You jerk, Lish!" she cried. "Did you hurt yourself badly?" she asked, trying to sound sympathetic.

"Not as badly as I'm going to hurt Esme."

"Esme?" Quinn repeated, shaking her head. "I'm mad at her too, for standing us up, but she couldn't help it that the Key West *Sassy* thing came through. And she did tell her mother to call us."

"But she didn't have to tempt Nicole into going with her," Alicia fumed.

Quinn shrugged and started to yank her mustache off as she led the way back to the dressing room. "You know our Esme. She definitely acts before she thinks. She probably forgot all about how Nicole was supposed to be in the play, too."

"Wonderful!" Alicia snapped in a rare burst of sarcasm. "And what a good friend Nicole is to go with her." Alicia stopped and helped Quinn unpin her brown wig.

Quinn stood with one hand on the door of the bathroom that had been transformed into a dressing room for the play. "It's definitely not like Nicole," Quinn mused, combing her fingers through her tangled red hair. "She's been acting so weird lately."

Alicia frowned. "Really. Nicole's usually a little weird around the holidays. I guess she gets so excited about seeing her dad, she totally spaces out."

Quinn put a warning hand on Alicia's arm. Cara and her buddies were sauntering down the hall in their direction. "Speaking of spacing out. I wish *we* could space out and conveniently forget about Knowles-It-All's party," Quinn whispered.

"Forget that, Q," Alicia declared firmly. "We decided to go and we have to stick with our decision. Besides, I don't want to give Cara and Co. the chance to badmouth your play behind your back—not tonight anyway."

"Okay, okay," Quinn agreed. "Maybe we'll get into a major food fight like last time, remember?"

Alicia giggled. Just thinking of the big rally Cara had thrown when she was running for class president, and how mad she'd been when it had turned into a huge food fight, with cake and sandwiches flying all over the place, always made Alicia crack up. Cara'd been even more angry when Alicia had won the election. "By the way, Quinno, the play was really great, and I'm so proud of you."

Quinn couldn't help beaming at the compliment. "You're just saying that 'cause you're my friend," she told Alicia. But even Jesse, Mimi, and Stephanie had praised her.

The Palms, the Knowles's estate, was ablaze with lights. Spaced every couple of feet, they made the driveway look like an airport runway. Chinese lanterns crisscrossed the sprawling backyard. Floodlights lit the area around the pool, and shadows danced in the mild breeze that was blowing off the ocean.

Alicia and Quinn carried plates heaped with tacos and salad over to some lounge chairs and collapsed against the cushions. "You'd think we'd had a Broadway opening or something—not just the annual Christmas pageant at the Swamp!" Quinn commented from her perch beneath a potted palm.

"I knew all along Cara should be the star," Jesse's voice piped up from nearby. "I told her so, too. Esme was just wrong for the role."

Quinn made a face in the dark. "Esme was perfect for the role, Jesse," she couldn't help interrupting. "She's a really good actress—a real pro—"

"Give me a break!" Cara cut in. "We know all about Esme's professional *acting* career," she continued smugly, as she smoothed an imaginary wrinkle out of her white minidress. She looked down her nose at Quinn, who was dressed in her favorite casual look—black baggy pants, cowboy boots, and a black-and-blue shirt that made her blue eyes look electric. "She really took Hollywood by storm." Cara went on, "Or should I say one man in Hollywood?"

"What happened with that weasely agent of hers has nothing to do with anything," Alicia screamed, jumping to Esme's defense. Esme had recently tried out for a film role, only to find out that her agent was a little bit of a sleaze. Somehow, the story had leaked out around school, and Cara had tried to make it sound as if the whole thing had been Esme's fault.

Quinn's blue eyes were blazing as she stared at Cara. "That's such old news, it predates Heartburn, you jerk!" Quinn exclaimed.

"Two points," Stephanie said, toasting Quinn with her Coke. "Meanwhile, what's with Nicole? Some friend she is to disappear like this!"

"Yeah, what happened to Miss Prep U.S.A.?" Jesse taunted.

Cara narrowed her eyes at Quinn. "Heartburn really has it in for her, you know."

"Thanks," Quinn said between gritted teeth, trying desperately to keep her cool. "I'll make sure to tell Nicole when I see her next."

Just then they heard someone yelling, "Is there a Quinn McNair or Alicia Antona here?"

"Yeah," Quinn yelled back, jumping up.

"There's a call for you. Long distance," the voice continued.

Alicia and Quinn walked through the French doors that opened onto the patio. Dora, the Knowles's maid, told them that if they both needed to talk, one of them could use the phone in the study and the other could use the one in the front hall.

"Finally!" Alicia murmured through clenched teeth. "*Now* Nicole calls."

"From Key West. That is long distance," Quinn reminded, as she lunged to pick up the phone.

Alicia hurried into the other room.

"Hello?"

"Quinn!" Esme's voice was so loud, Quinn jumped.

"Esme, you don't have to yell just 'cause it's long distance!"

On the other end of the line, Esme sighed. "Don't be mad," Esme implored in her sweetest voice.

"*Mad* is not the word," Alicia shouted from the study at such a volume Quinn had to pull the receiver away from her ear. "Furious is more like it."

"Somewhat ready to kill," Quinn added. "We're thinking of forming our own special SWAT team to do you in, Es."

Esme giggled. "Come on, guys. Think of the bright side. If I had been there, Cara would never have had to be the bag lady. How did it go? I'm dying," Esme continued breathlessly.

"Pretty good, considering," Quinn said coolly.

"Considering what?"

"Considering you not only had to take off for a glamorous modeling shoot the day of our little play—" Alicia cut in before Esme could utter one word of protest. "But to talk Nicole into going to Key West with you. That was pretty sneaky—"

"And very inconsiderate," Quinn added.

"What are you talking about?" Esme sounded surprised. "Is it the connection, or did I hear you say something about Nicole?"

"Bag it, Cornflake," Quinn growled. "We're in no mood for your spacy act. Why in the world did you take Nicole down there with you?"

There was a silence on the other end of the phone. "Nicole's *not* with me," Esme said quietly, in a very small voice.

"Where is she then?" Alicia asked angrily. "Down at the docks doing some moonlight fishing?"

"I . . . I don't know what you're talking about," Esme replied in the same quiet, frightened voice.

"Stop it, Lish," Quinn said, cocking her head to one side. "You're serious, Esme. Nicole really isn't with you?"

"Nope."

"Ayyyye!" Alicia wailed. "But her grandmother

thinks she is. She told us so. She wasn't here for the play. Quinn had to take Nicole's place at the last minute. What happened to her?" Alicia cried out hysterically.

"Calm down," Esme commanded in the serious voice she almost never used. "I have a feeling I know exactly what happened to her."

"What?!" the other girls chorused.

"The stables," Esme whispered. "Candy's mare. Was Candy at the play?"

Quinn slapped her forehead. "No, come to think of it. Esme, you are brilliant sometimes. Really brilliant."

"I bet the mare had its baby—" Esme said.

"Foal," Alicia corrected.

"And that's where Nicole is. You know how her mother and her grandparents are about her hanging out at the stables all the time. She probably sneaked out and told her grandmother she'd be with me to get her off her back. She had no way of knowing I wouldn't be around since my agent called at the last minute."

"Don't worry," Quinn hastened to reassure Esme. "We'll cover for her."

They said good-bye to Esme. Alicia met Quinn outside the study. Quinn started back down the hall toward the party, but Alicia stopped her.

"We have to go see for ourselves," Alicia said gravely.

"See what, Lish?"

"If Nicole really is at the stables. If she isn't . . ."

Quinn laughed at Alicia's dramatics. "You've been watching too many horror movies again. I can always tell 'cause your eyes start to bug out."

Alicia went to look at herself in the mirror above the phone stand. "My eyes look like they always do," she muttered.

"Nothing's happened to Nicole, Lish. She's at the stables. It's the only thing that makes sense. And Nicole never does things that don't make sense."

"Still—I think we should go over there."

"When?"

Alicia frowned. "Now, I guess. But how?"

"My bike is back at school," Quinn said.

"Mine, too," Alicia put in. Suddenly she brightened. "We'll take the bus. It stops at the end of Ponce de Leon Boulevard." She checked her watch. "It's not even seven yet. The bus is still running."

The two girls turned on their heels, leaving the noise of the party behind them. They crept out the front door and down the long, palm-lined driveway to the street.

CHAPTER 8

By the time the bus stopped in front of Palm Beach Prep, it was packed with Christmas shoppers. Quinn and Alicia pushed their way out, and hurried through the wrought-iron gates that flanked the school's entrance. Cars still dotted the parking lot and lights were on in the main building, but it was still pretty creepy.

"I can see it now," Alicia whispered in Quinn's ear. "The ghost of that girl who disappeared in the swamp is coming to get us, her bloody hands outstretched—"

"Stop it," Quinn commanded. "It's creepy enough without your horror stories."

"At least people are still around," Alicia said, voicing Quinn's own opinion. Quinn hadn't exactly relished the idea of going back to find the main building deserted. Quinn was used to breaking rules, but hanging out on PBP property when school was closed seemed like an open invitation for Heartburn to put her on probation.

"The maintenance people and those volunteers from the Royal Poinciana Theater must be cleaning up the auditorium," Quinn guessed.

She and Alicia stopped to get their bikes from the rack. They put on their headlamps, and rode behind the school down the well-lit path toward the stables.

"Look!" Quinn shouted as they cycled up in front. The stable doors were open and a square of light spilled out onto the sandy ground. The animal-hospital van was parked next to Candy Gordon's red Alfa. Quinn braked quickly, sending a shower of gravel and dust up from the path. She looked over her shoulder at Alicia, a smug expression on her face.

"They're obviously in the stable now," Quinn pointed out. "Esme was right. Of course, Nicole is here with the vet and Candy. Ginger probably had her foal, so Nicole snuck out of the house today just to come here," she continued patiently.

Alicia chose to ignore Quinn's smug attitude, and was instead more happy that Nicole was really okay. *"Bueno!"* Alicia exclaimed, as she straddled her bike and adjusted the straps on her red cotton overalls. "You were right. I'm so so so glad, you know. Still," Alicia frowned. "It's so not like Nicole not to call us," she continued in concern.

Quinn blew her bangs off her forehead and snickered. "Can you imagine Nicole calling and saying she was sorry about bagging out of the play, but she had to see Ginger's foal!"

Alicia laughed at the thought. "*Ay*! I would have told here where to go. Then I would have hauled her kicking and screaming, over to the auditorium." Alicia paused and giggled some more. "I'm still mad at her, but at least we know she's all right."

Alicia laughed again, then nervously eyed the open stable entrance. "Do we have to go in?" She lived in dire fear of horses and the idea of getting close to them always got her a little crazed.

"Of course, weenie-face. Nicole's not getting away with this. We were really worried." Quinn leaned her ten-speed against the fence and started for the stable. She turned to Alicia and winked. "Besides, I wouldn't miss seeing this foal for the world."

"I knew you'd say that," Alicia muttered, as she jammed her hands into her overall pockets and reluctantly followed Quinn through the door. Unlike Alicia, Quinn wasn't afraid of horses at all, even though her only experience with them before this fall had been on merry-go-rounds.

The two girls tiptoed into the stable. They poked their heads around the corner and spotted

Candy Gordon. The tall blond riding instructor was standing next to Dr. Grossman, the vet. They were both sipping coffee from Styrofoam cups. Candy was gazing into Ginger's stall and beaming.

"It was just like watching a human baby being born," Candy said in a voice so soft and silly that Alicia had to clamp her hand over her mouth not to laugh.

Quinn edged a bit closer. Alicia crept up behind her, managing to keep Quinn between herself and the stall where the horses were.

"You've got a winner on your hands!" Dr. Grossman said proudly. Before he could say anything else, he noticed the two girls peering shyly around the corner of the stall.

"Gosh, I never thought horses started out *that* small," Quinn said, her voice full of wonder.

"Quinn? Alicia?" Candy exclaimed, looking at them in surprise. The happy expression on her face turned slowly into a frown. "What are *you* doing here? And where, may I ask, is Nicole? I called her the minute I found Ginger in labor."

"*Madre Mía!*" Alicia gasped. She looked at Quinn in total alarm. Quinn returned her stare, looking horrified.

"Uh . . . well, I don't really know," Quinn said slowly. "We thought she might be here, but I guess she's . . ." For the first time in her life, Quinn was at a loss for words. She was afraid to admit that no one knew where Nicole was. It might get her friend into a lot of trouble.

Alicia toyed with one of her red plastic earrings. She sighed heavily. "Candy," Alicia said in a very small voice, "we don't know where Nicole is, and we're worried."

Dr. Grossman eyed Alicia. "Worried?"

Quinn nodded. "She never showed for the play. And she didn't call anyone." Quinn's voice shook a little, even though she was trying to be calm. "We thought she was with Esme but Esme said she'd be here with you."

Candy pursed her lips, deep in thought. Then, she began to smile. "There's no mystery, girls. I think I know exactly what's going on." She dusted her hands off on the legs of her jeans, and strode over to the row of hooks outside the tack room. She grabbed her jacket and slipped it on. "She's with her mother, of course. That's got to be it." Candy popped a stick of gum into her mouth and stretched to work out a kink in her neck. "With all these wedding plans—"

"*Wedding!*" Alicia and Quinn exclaimed in unison. "What wedding?!"

"*Caramba!*" Alicia cried. "How dumb can we be!" She grabbed Quinn and shook her. "Remember—the Mouse—Wednesday night—the big dinner at the Breakers—"

"And Nicole had to go with her mother and that guy, Abe something," Quinn continued.

"Adam Stanton, you mean," Candy corrected with a laugh.

"How come you knew about this?" Quinn sputtered. "And we're Nicole's best friends in the whole world, and we didn't even know."

"Really," Alicia echoed.

"Nicole didn't tell me, girls. Mrs. Hartman did," Candy explained.

"I don't get it," Quinn cut in. "How come everyone knew about Mrs. Whitcomb marrying the Mouse except us?"

This time, Candy was taken aback. "The Mouse?" she asked, surprised. "I've met Adam Stanton before. He happens to be a very nice man, and not mousy at all."

Quinn scuffed her cowboy boots in the dust. She was trying very hard not to laugh.

"Well, he is sort of bald, you know," Alicia explained lamely. "I can't imagine marrying someone with no hair."

Dr. Grossman patted his own balding head and sighed. "I think that's my cue to go."

Candy and the girls laughed, as they walked him to the door.

"About Adam Stanton," Candy said, breathing deeply after Dr. Grossman had pulled out. "I think he may be just what the doctor ordered." She leaned back against the doorframe and looked thoughtful.

For a minute, Quinn thought Candy was talking about Dr. Grossman and Ginger.

"Nicole's mother will probably be home more, now that she's remarrying and Adam is moving to Palm Beach. And I think he'll make a good stepfather for Nicole."

Alicia's head snapped up. *"Ay!"* she muttered. "A *stepfather.*" She caught Quinn's eye, and nodded toward their bikes.

Quinn got the hint. "Well, Candy, I guess we'd better get going now."

"Back to Cara's party?" Candy asked, checking her watch. "It's probably still in full swing."

"We might just ride back to Alicia's now. We're halfway there," Quinn said, anxious to hear what her friend was thinking.

Alicia pedaled quickly out to the street, and then stopped beneath a street lamp. She turned to Quinn. Her face was pale.

"No way is Nicole with her mother," Alicia said seriously.

"How do you know?"

"Because her grandmother would have told us that. Instead, she told us Nicole was with Esme." Alicia stopped.

"But she isn't and . . ." Quinn's voice trailed off as understanding hit her. "She really is missing."

"It's this whole wedding thing. And the Mouse.

She probably freaked when she found out her mother was going to marry the guy." Alicia's voice began to shake. "I'm scared, Quinn. I think we should tell her grandmother or someone. She could be in trouble."

Quinn thought over what Alicia had just said very carefully. "Yeah, maybe. But, let's try to retrace her steps first. What exactly did her grandmother tell you on the phone?"

"That she was with Esme!" Alicia was impatient. "I told you that already."

"Yeah, yeah," Quinn murmured, distracted. She leaned over the handlebars of her bike and gnawed her lip. "Is that *all* she said?"

"Yeah, and that Nicole took her bike and went to Esme's for the weekend."

"Her bike!" Quinn slapped her hand against her leg. "All right, Lish. Let's retrace her steps. Maybe she really did go to Esme's. We'll ask Esme's mother where Nicole put her bike. Maybe she knows something."

"And if she doesn't?"

Quinn tried not to look too grim. "Then we'll tell her what's going on. She'll know what to do."

When they got to Esme's, Quinn pounded on the door for what seemed like forever. "Where could Esme's mom be?" she finally asked, turning to Alicia.

Alicia was pacing back and forth on the porch. "I don't know. Hey, I just remembered. Her mom isn't home. She's at a convention."

"That's right," Quinn nodded. "Esme told us last week that her mother might not make the play, unless she could get to Tampa and back in one day. Her mom was all upset about missing Esme in a starring role, too."

Quinn blew out her breath, and stood tapping her foot against the porch floor. "Well, we've followed Nicole's steps this far, but now what?"

The headlights of a passing car reflected off something metallic half buried in the bushes behind Esme's garage. Alicia jumped off the porch and hurried over to get a better look.

"Quinn," she yelled moments later. "It's here. It's Nicole's bike. I'd know it anywhere."

Alicia stood the blue bike up. Its white seat and white-taped handlebars clearly identified it as Nicole's. "Quinn, she's been here!" Alicia sounded amazed.

Quinn's face was serious. "And she lost this somehow." Quinn pulled a yellow "I love La-La land" scarf off a branch, where it was snagged.

Alicia slowly shook her head as she gazed at the scarf. "Oh, Quinn," she wailed. "Something awful's happened to Nicole. I feel it, here." She tapped her heart emphatically with one finger, as a few tears trickled down her cheeks.

Quinn wanted to tell Alicia she was overreacting, but she couldn't. A terrible thought had just occurred to her. "Lish, I'm worried. Nicole's family is very rich and, well, very high society. Maybe she's been kidnapped . . ."

CHAPTER 9

Key West was overcrowded, and it looked like all anyone wanted to do was have fun. At least that's what Nicole thought after walking up and down the bustling streets for what seemed like hours. Nicole had always hated parties. Parties meant lots of people—crowds of people all crunched together in one place at one particular time. Nicole liked people in ones and twos, never more than threes. Sometimes, she thought she was happiest alone with her horse, Simon. There didn't seem to be any place she could be alone in Key West. Although the air smelled sweet, and the ocean was very inviting, she didn't like it here very much at all.

When she squinted hard enough into the lingering half-light that followed sunset, Nicole could just make out the outline of a bird at the end of the pier. It was perched on top of a piling, and from its shape she guessed it was a heron. Nicole was a whiz at birds and animals in general. She just wasn't very good at people. If she could just walk up to that bird and ask if the *Starry Night* was docked somewhere nearby, her life would be so much simpler.

Nicole felt totally lost, and realized that she had to work up the nerve to ask somebody if they knew where her father was. She took a deep breath. The savory scent of something yummy filled her nostrils, and her tummy rumbled loudly. She dug her hand into the pocket of her jeans. Her carefully folded five-dollar bill was still there, and she still had fourteen dollars and seventy-five cents left in her wallet. Well, she didn't have to pay for a hotel that night, and hoped she would find her dad sometime the next day.

"I really shouldn't starve myself," she murmured, figuring that she could afford to spend at least a couple of dollars on something to eat, suddenly realizing that she hadn't eaten all day. She sniffed the air again and followed her nose to a small storefront. A white wooden sign that read "Skipper's Victuals and Nauticals," upon which an impossibly fat parrot's outline was sketched in green, caught Nicole's eye as it swayed back and forth in the breeze. Another sign in the window read "clam bar."

This must be a place where sailors hang out, Nicole thought, as she pushed open the screen door and slowly walked in. Dolly Parton's voice poured out of the jukebox, and posters and signed photos of the country singer were plastered all over the walls. The room was almost deserted. There were a few glass-topped tables with blue-checked place mats, but Nicole didn't see anyone eating.

It was kind of eerie inside, since it was the first place she had seen in Key West that wasn't jam-packed with tourists. One wall held a display case filled with nautical instruments, some of them vaguely familiar to Nicole from the short time she'd spent on her dad's boat last summer. The other wall was devoted to a grill and service counter.

Nicole turned and noticed a wiry man behind the counter. Thick gray hair poked out every which way from under his beaked sea-captain's cap. But Nicole's eyes passed quickly over the man and riveted on his shoulder, where a fat, colorful parrot stared intently in her direction.

"Hallo sailor!" said the parrot in a decidedly Cuban accent.

Nicole giggled, and stuttered in a quiet voice, "Uh—hi."

"May I help you, miss?" the man asked. He smiled and the million or so wrinkles around his eyes deepened.

"I . . . I," Nicole glanced quickly at the menu board hanging on the wall. "I'll take a shrimp roll, please, and some fries."

"Coming right up!" said the parrot.

Nicole laughed again. "It's hard to tell who's talking," she said, leaning towards the parrot. She'd never owned a bird, although once she'd nursed a fledgling woodpecker she had found in her yard. She sat down on one of the swivel stools in front of the counter and hooked her feet over the rungs.

"Don't much matter," the man said. "Dirty Harry here and me—we go back a long way together."

"Are you Skipper, like it says on the sign?" Nicole asked bravely. For the first time in her life she found it easy talking to a stranger. Something about the man's eyes made her trust him. It actually felt good to talk to someone again.

"The very one," he announced, laughing. "And how'd you end up here In Key West? Are you on vacation with your parents?" he asked.

Nicole took a deep breath. Somehow, she didn't want to lie to this man. She hesitated, deciding what to say. "I'm looking for someone," she finally said. "Actually, for a boat."

Skipper eyed her carefully. "Ain't you a little young to travel alone?" he questioned.

Nicole swallowed hard. She was afraid to tell the truth but she hated to lie. "I'm looking for the *Starry Night*. I heard it's about to dock here for repairs. The Captain—"

"Chris Whitcomb!" The way Skipper said his name made Nicole realize he must know her father. "A great guy. You know him?"

Nicole didn't answer yes or no, so it wasn't really lying when she answered, "I'm supposed to interview him for my school newspaper."

"So you're here with a school group," Skipper said, nodding his approval.

"Hate school!" squawked Dirty Harry.

Nicole arched her eyebrows. "When did you go to school?" she asked the bird.

"Hate school!" Dirty Harry repeated, and then let out a long string of words that more than explained how he got his name.

Skipper looked embarrassed. "Don't know where he picked that one up," he muttered. He turned back to the grill and drained Nicole's fries. A moment later, he placed a plate heaped with food in front of her.

"Yep," he said, leaning on the counter as he filled his pipe with tobacco. "I heard the *Starry Night* put into port about an hour ago."

Nicole stopped mid-bite. "It did?" she practically shrieked. Her stomach tightened and her heart started beating quickly. "Where is it?" she demanded, as she wiped her mouth with a napkin and jumped off the stool.

"Hey, slow down, missy. No one'd be on board

tonight," the old skipper chuckled. "But I could take you to see her tomorrow if ya' want."

Nicole's heart sank. She was so close. Her father was somewhere in this town—right down the block, for all she knew. But Nicole had no way of finding out where.

She sat down again, and forced herself to eat. After a moment she asked, "Will my—will the captain be there for sure? Tomorrow, I mean."

"Yep," Skipper nodded, sensing Nicole's disappointment.

"Harry hungry!" the parrot squawked, sounding pathetic.

Skipper rolled his eyes. "You need food like a hole in the head," he complained, but reached under the counter and held out his hand under the bird's curved beak. Daintily the green-and-orange creature pecked up some seeds.

"So where are you staying with your group?" Skipper asked.

Nicole told him, and reached in her pocket for her money. "I'd better head back there," she said. "I want to get down here early to find my—I mean the captain."

Skipper looked at her curiously. "Wouldn't try before noon," he advised. "The repair crew will be crawling all over the *Starry Night* until then. Captain Chris won't be in the mood for an interview with *that* bunch around. Then, of course, they're scheduled to pull out of port around two."

"That soon?" Nicole cried out, horrified. She felt her eyes begin to tingle, the way they did when she was about to cry. She'd barely have time to talk to her dad before he went out to sea again. She had a funny feeling she'd need some time to convince him to take her on board.

"If you're headed back to the Coral Grove," Skipper began, interrupting Nicole's thoughts, "I'll give you a lift. My truck's right outside, and there's not much business tonight." He eyed the empty room. "Not many ships around this week," he said, and added, with a chuckle, "and I can't see too many of those tourists roughing it with Skipper's Victuals."

Nicole agreed readily, putting all her trust in the old sailor. She watched Dirty Harry hop on the man's shoulder, and together they headed down the block to where his truck was parked, just outside a sidewalk cafe.

"I really appreciate this, Mr.—" Nicole suddenly realized she didn't even know his name.

He laughed. "Just Skipper," he said. "That's how everyone around here knows me. Just plain old Skipper."

He turned on the ignition and they pulled out into the traffic. Instantly, the light turned red. While they were stopped, Nicole looked out the open window. A group of girls were laughing really loud at one of the round white tables in front of the Conch Shell Cafe. Nicole looked past them. On the corner, a slender blond girl in long white Jams and a striped baggy shirt was standing in an open phone booth. She had one hand over her ear and was talking rapidly into the receiver.

The light changed. The truck started up with a jerk. Skipper's hand shot out to steady Nicole. "You okay?" he asked, firmly gripping her shoulder.

She couldn't answer. She sort of nodded, then looked quickly back out the window. "Esme?" she gasped, suddenly recognizing the blond.

Nicole slumped down in her seat. Key West was not a very big place. How was she supposed to keep on avoiding Esme? What if Esme had just seen her? What would she think, seeing Nicole in a red truck with an old man and a parrot? Nicole wouldn't know how to explain. Could she ever trust Esme to keep her secret about moving in with her father?

CHAPTER 10

While Nicole was being driven safely back to her hotel in Key West, Alicia and Quinn, back in Palm Beach, were nervously trying to decide what to do. Alicia sat cross-legged on her bed, surrounded by a mountain of colorful throw pillows. She held her hot-pink, plastic phone in her lap, and looked expectantly at Quinn.

Quinn was pacing the floor. It took five long strides to reach the French doors that opened onto the balcony of Alicia's room. It was four strides back to the white wicker desk. Alicia sat, drumming her fingers nervously on the phone, as she kept her eyes focused on Quinn.

Halfway to the balcony, Quinn stopped. She turned on her heels. "Okay," she said confidently. "There's no other choice. We'll call the police—now!"

Alicia winced. "I have bad vibes about the police," she said. She didn't know why, but she had a definite feeling that getting the police involved was the *wrong* thing to do. Then again, she thought, maybe calling the police was the *only* thing to do. She cradled the phone in her lap and ran her hands nervously through her thick, wild curls. She looked up at Quinn with dark, troubled eyes.

"I guess we should," Alicia said quietly, not sounding very definite at all. Suddenly, she felt no older than her eleven years, and very young and inexperienced. Quinn looked at her questioningly.

"But," Alicia defended herself, "on '21 Jump Street' last week, they said the police don't think a person is missing unless they haven't been seen for at least twenty-four hours."

That stopped Quinn. "Hmmm. We don't *know* exactly how long Nicole's been gone, but I haven't heard from her since yesterday, during rehearsal. And then she pulled her vanishing act this afternoon. She *could* have been gone for twenty-four hours already," Quinn figured quickly. "She could have been kidnapped last night."

"We aren't *sure* she's been kidnapped," Alicia jumped in quickly.

"Alicia!" Quinn practically yelled, running out of patience. "Look! *First* of all, we found her bike. *Second,* we found her scarf—there was probably some sort of struggle—" Quinn suggested ominously, letting her imagination take over. "*Third,* Nicole just does *not* do things like this. She wouldn't just vanish into thin air. She's a Whitcomb. They play by the rules."

Alicia looked morose. "I guess you're right," she muttered. Reluctantly she added, "We probably don't have a minute to lose."

Alicia had actually dialed the 9 in 9-1-1, when Quinn grabbed the receiver from her hand and hung it up again.

"Let's try her house—just one more time," Quinn suggested. The idea of speaking to the police was pretty scary.

Just then, the phone rang. Both girls reached for it. Alicia got there first and Quinn ran to pick up the hallway extension.

"Nicole?" Alicia was the first to speak.

"Uh—no. Just me."

"Esme!" the girls groaned.

On the other end of the phone, Esme's face fell. "Gee, sorry to disappoint you," she said quietly. "But I just wondered if you had found Nicole yet." She bit her lip. "And I guess that means you *haven't.*"

Esme fiddled with the hem of her skirt. She rocked back and forth on her heels. Beneath her mop of blond curls, her high forehead was wrinkled in a frown.

"You guys, I'm *sooo* worried!" she said in a crackly voice, and her friends could tell she was close to tears.

"So are we, *Carina,*" Alicia said. "We just don't know what to do." Alicia told Esme about the search for Nicole, and how they had found her bike in Esme's yard.

"And the scarf, too," Quinn added darkly. "Someone's kidnapped her for sure."

"KIDNAPPED!!!" Esme howled into the phone. "Oh my gosh!" She held the receiver hard in both hands. Suddenly, she was distracted by someone walking behind her, carrying a portable radio, turned up to full volume. Esme turned around and glared at the guy's back. "What do we do?" she breathed into the phone.

"We're going to call her house one more time. If no one answers, we'll *have* to call the police," Quinn explained. "But we don't want to call the police unless we're really, really sure." Alicia couldn't believe how calm Quinn was being.

"The police?" Esme sounded shocked. She certainly hadn't thought of going to the police. Just then, something caught Esme's eye. "Hey—wait a minute." She squinted. Across the street from the phone booth, she saw a rusted, red truck. It had stopped for the light.

"Quinn—" Esme's voice sank to a whisper. "Omygosh."

"Es, are you okay?" Alicia looked at the receiver. "What's happening?"

"You're *right*!" she cried out. The horror in Esme's voice was unmistakable. "Nicole *has* been kidnapped. And they've taken her—omygosh—they're pulling off. She's in a truck with a terrible-looking old man—" Esme squeaked. "He's got a PARROT!" she cried out, but she wasn't holding the phone anymore. She had dropped the receiver and bolted down the block after the truck. She wanted to at least try to get a look at the license plate.

"ESME!! Where are you???" Quinn shouted into the phone. Alicia's hand clapped quickly over Quinn's mouth.

"Is something wrong, girls?" Mr. Antona called from the living room.

Alicia put a finger to her lips, and gave Quinn a warning. Then she ran out to the hall and yelled, "*Nada, Papa.*"

Quinn was amazed at how calm Alicia managed to sound. "What do you mean, '*nothing*'?" Quinn was on her feet now. "Esme just saw Nicole in Key West. She was being—being shoved into some sort of car with a man. NO!" Quinn looked a little wild-eyed. "A truck. She said it was a truck." Quinn shuddered to think of well-bred, gentle-mannered Nicole being shoved into anything, let alone a dingy, dirty old truck. "Alicia Antona, *how* can you say nothing's *wrong*? I think we should tell your parents exactly what's going on and—"

"Shut up!" Alicia commanded in her best class-president's voice. "And listen. I will not call anyone or tell anyone *anything* until we think about this some more!"

"Am I hearing straight?" Quinn gaped at Alicia in disbelief. "Wouldn't you know it? Alicia Antona is controlling herself in the middle of a *real* emergency."

Alicia's voice actually shook as she slowly replied, "I am *not* calm!" Then she took a deep breath, as she continued, "I am anything but calm, but *chica,* listen to me. I have a feeling I know exactly what happened, and if we tell anyone—*anyone* at all—we could make a whole lot of trouble for Nicole."

"How much more trouble can she get into? I mean it's dark out, she's hundreds of miles from home. She's alone—actually, worse than alone." Quinn's voice trailed off miserably. "She's with a dangerous man!"

"Quinn McNair, will you *listen* to me?" Alicia demanded, raising her voice to try to get Quinn to stop talking. "I think you're letting your imagination run away with you again. This is not one of your adventure stories, Q. I said I think I know what happened to Nicole. I think she's with her father."

"Her *father*?" Quinn blinked. "Why would her father—"

"Kidnap her?" Alicia finished for her friend. "Because Nicole and her dad are very close. They always have been. Ever since the divorce, Nicole almost never gets to see him—two, maybe three times a year. If he's heard that Mrs. Whitcomb is getting remarried, who knows what—"

Quinn's face lit up as she suddenly realized what was going on. "And now he kidnaps her— I've read about stuff like that. The parents who don't have custody of their kids after a divorce steal them away from the parents who do."

"Exactly!" Alicia bobbed her curls vigorously. "Even some of the missing children you hear about are kids just like that—just like Nicole."

Quinn propped her chin on her knees and thought over what Alicia said. Then, with a brisk shake of her head, she suddenly declared, "But it's still wrong. We *should* call the police. Mrs. Whitcomb must be worried sick. Maybe she's called them already."

Alicia laughed sadly and said, "Nicole's mother probably doesn't even know she's gone. Remember the answering machine—she won't be home until the day after tomorrow." After a moment she added, "Besides, Nicole is nuts about her dad. She adores him and definitely wants to be just like him. If we get the police involved then her dad might get in big trouble, too. Nicole would hate that!"

Quinn nodded slowly. "I don't like it, but you're right," she agreed with her friend. "Still, Lish," she continued, "we've got to do something." Quinn was back on her feet. She shoved her hands in the back pockets of her pants and narrowed her eyes. "We can't just let her vanish like this and not try to help."

"If only we could *talk* to her," Alicia mused. "I'm sure we could persuade her that she belongs back with her mother, even if Mrs. Whitcomb is marrying that man Nicole calls the Mouse."

Quinn looked up sharply. "Talk to her?" she repeated very slowly. "Alicia," she shrieked, grabbing her friend by the shoulders and shaking her hard. "You're a genius."

"*Ay,* I feel a McNair plan coming on," Alicia murmured, sounding worried. "I'm not sure I'm going to like it."

"Don't you see," Quinn started talking really fast. "We *will* talk to her. We'll go down to Key West tomorrow and try to talk some sense into her. I'm sure we can persuade her to escape from her father and come back with us!" Quinn's eyes were dancing at the prospect of adventure. "I'm sure it'll be easy to find her father there. I mean you heard the news story—it said that his boat was docked there for repairs."

She looked thoughtful for a moment before continuing, "I'll bet there was nothing wrong with his ship in the first place. He probably just flew up here, got Nicole, and whisked her off to Key West." Quinn, who planned to be a writer when she was older, grew really excited as she imagined all the details of Nicole's kidnapping. It was almost fun, now that she was sure Nicole was with her dad, and probably quite safe. "What a great story it makes!" she couldn't help adding.

Alicia gave Quinn a disgusted look. "It might make a very *sad* story when Nicole's mother finds out. And she's sure to figure out something happened to Nicole sooner or later."

Quinn frowned. "Oh, why didn't we think of this earlier? We could have left for Key West today. But it's definitely already too late tonight, and—"

"Hold it, Q. Are you absolutely *loco*?" Alicia cried, angrily. "My father will *never* let me go to Key West with you!"

"My parents would kill me, too," Quinn agreed, but she didn't seem at all fazed by that prospect. "We just won't tell them exactly where we're going."

"Quinn," Alicia warned. "We're going to get in really big trouble if they ever find out, you know."

"But they won't find out," Quinn said smugly.

"I've got the perfect plan." She got up and walked over to the phone, as she continued, "Let me call the depot and see what time buses leave for Key West."

"And how much they cost," Alicia added, frowning because, once again, she was agreeing to a crazy Quinn McNair plan. She walked over to her desk and pulled out the red-and-black lacquered box her parents had brought her back last year from their tour of China. She opened it, and dumped a wad of bills and some change onto her bed. While Alicia counted the money, her friend called the bus station.

A few minutes later, Quinn had all the information she needed. The fare was thirty-four dollars one way. The first bus left a little after five o'clock the next morning, and it was the only express bus scheduled for that day, due to arrive in Key West before noon.

"How do we get back?" Alicia asked, as she counted out seventy-four dollars. It was just enough to get them there, with a few dollars to spare.

Quinn turned the pockets of her jeans inside out. She had ten dollars and thirty-seven cents. "We'll think of something. Maybe I could call Sean from Key West. He's sure to have some money he can wire to us."

"Why don't we just ask him now?" Alicia wondered.

"We can't call him from here," Quinn answered quickly. "He would *never* let us go. Sometimes I think he's more protective than Mom and Dad."

"Okay," Alicia agreed. "But haven't you forgotten one small detail?"

Quinn looked up, surprised. She was sure she had thought of everything. "What detail?" she asked.

"Our parents!" Alicia cried. She doubted that even Quinn could think of a way for them to sneak out of town without either set of parents knowing. Alicia's father, having raised three older daughters, knew all the tricks, and was especially strict with her because she was the youngest.

"Piece of cake!" Quinn grinned, and picked up the phone again. "Listen," she mouthed to Alicia. When Mrs. McNair answered the phone, Quinn told her that she'd be staying over at Alicia's for the rest of the weekend.

Then she turned back to Alicia. "Now," she instructed, "you tell your dad you're staying at my place. When he thinks we've left the apartment, we sneak back in here, and climb into bed, and get some sleep. We've got to get out of here early enough tomorrow to catch the five o'clock bus."

"The what?" Alicia's mouth fell open. According to Alicia, no one in their right mind ever got out of bed before ten a.m. on weekends. She personally preferred sleeping until noon. "Quinn, that's practically the middle of the night," she grumbled. "*Caramba*! We might as well stay up and watch the 'Saturday Night Horror Marathon' on Channel Three."

Quinn agreed that would be fun, but then was serious. "Except," she added, trying to be sensible, "we should start out rested. Adventures always start at the crack of dawn after a good night's sleep."

"Dawn," Alicia mumbled. "That's a dirty word around this house. And besides, at five a.m. the week before Christmas, it's still pitch-black," Alicia pointed out. "Dark. You know? I mean dark, as in the middle of the N-I-G-H-T!" Alicia spelled out the word just so Quinn would get the point.

But it was no use. Quinn had already made up her mind, and there was definitely no changing it!

CHAPTER 11

By the time Esme dragged herself down to the Coral Grove dining room the next morning, Nicole had long since fled her "borrowed" hotel room, and Quinn and Alicia were halfway to Key West. Esme was the last model to take a seat. Pitchers of juice, plates of *croissants* and hot *pain-au-chocolats* were in the middle of the table for the hotel's famous, family-style breakfast. She couldn't believe that *Sassy* had allowed the models on the shoot to be given such fattening foods. Usually, she was offered a piece of fruit or some plain, low-fat yogurt.

"Esme, didn't you look at your schedule?" scolded Sarah Wood. She poured Esme a glass of freshly squeezed orange juice, and handed her a warm *pain-au-chocolat*. "You're due for makeup and hair in exactly twenty minutes down at the trailer in Mallory Square." She leaned forward across the table and took a good look at Esme. "Are you all right?" she asked, and felt Esme's forehead with her hand.

"Girl, you've got circles under your eyes that go right down to your chin!" commented another model, Kesia Murphy. Esme and Kesia had worked together on lots of shoots recently, and although Kesia was already sixteen, she and Esme were becoming friends.

"I'm fine!" Esme said testily, and shoved her hands into the pockets of her baggy purple shorts. "It's just that sometimes it's just hard to sleep when I'm away from home," she mumbled. Actually, Esme usually slept like a log anywhere, anytime. In fact, Nicole was always teasing her about their disastrous fourth-grade trip to Sea World, in Orlando. For some reason, the buses had forgotten to pick up the girls to take them back to Palm Beach and they had been forced to wait for three hours in a dirty waiting room. Esme had simply found a bench at the back of the room and quickly fallen asleep. In fact, Esme didn't even wake up when the buses finally arrived and all the other girls got up to go. Nicole had to run back to wake her up. Esme wasn't fazed in the least. She had just gotten on the bus with Nicole, fallen back to sleep, and stayed that way until they arrived in Palm Beach. Esme thought of Nicole, and her eyes brimmed with tears. She was so worried because she was absolutely positive that Nicole had been kidnapped by that horrible-looking, bearded man. The night before, Esme had actually run five whole blocks trying to keep his red truck in sight, but at a busy intersection she had lost it. Now, all she could think about was Nicole tied up in some dockside warehouse, being held for ransom. Two tears trickled down her cheeks. She rubbed them away with the back of her hand. She felt so helpless and confused. She wondered if maybe she should call the police, even though Alicia and Quinn had told her not to.

"Hey, are you homesick, girl?" Kesia asked softly, as she passed Esme a tissue under the table.

Esme cast her friend a grateful look. "Yeah. I guess that's it." She blew her nose. Somehow she had to find Nicole. Worse yet, she had tried to call Quinn that morning to ask her about calling the police, but her mother said she was at Alicia's for the weekend. When she had called the Antonas', however, Alicia's sister Carla said Alicia was spending the rest of the weekend at Quinn's. Esme had hung up frightened. Obviously her friends were up to something—Quinn probably had some hare-brained scheme to track down Nicole. Were they going to get themselves into trouble too?

Part of Esme was relieved at the thought that

maybe her friends were headed down to Key West. She hadn't known Quinn McNair all that long, but she had great confidence that her friend could tackle almost any problem that came her way. After all, she had tackled awful Cara Knowles during her first week at Palm Beach Prep and survived that very well!

But another part of Esme was scared. Alicia and Quinn hadn't seen the creepy old man who had kidnapped Nicole. Cara was nothing compared to him. And they hadn't seen that horrible parrot, all orange-and-green and weird-looking. Esme shuddered and tried hard to swallow the rest of her juice. For some reason, Esme found the parrot particularly threatening.

"So are you up to working the shoot today?" Sarah asked, startling Esme.

"Working?" Esme straightened up in her chair. Never, ever, had she cancelled out on a shoot. Her friends might think she was an absolute flake, but when it came to her modeling career, Esme Farrell was a real pro. "Of course I can work. I'm here, aren't I? I just didn't sleep well."

"A little makeup and no one will notice," Kesia commented.

Esme got up and followed the other girls out to the minivan parked in the hotel driveway. She wouldn't miss this shoot for the world. Besides, being out and around in the old part of

Key West would put her closer to the docks and warehouses, the likeliest places in this town for kidnappers to stow their victims. She was sure she'd be able to keep one eye peeled for Nicole.

Makeup, and the brilliant sunshine glistening off the white buildings near the pier, did wonders for Esme. So did the fact that her cute miniskirt version of a sailor suit was attracting a lot of attention from people watching the shoot. In the broad light of day, she felt more confident that Nicole would be okay. The photographer posed the girls in front of one of the piers. Behind them, pelicans dove into the water, and pink birds soared through the air. Esme felt happier at the sight of them, and the photographer zoomed in for a picture of her smile.

During the break, Esme sauntered over to a vending machine. She had just put a second quarter in when an orange-and-green flash of color caught her eye. She shoved her heart-shaped sunglasses up on her nose to get a better look. "It's him!" she gasped, spotting the sailor with the parrot. This time he had Nicole by the arm, and was quickly guiding her down the street toward a more rundown part of town. Nicole had to rush to keep up with him.

Esme frantically looked for help, but there were no policemen in sight. Without a moment's hesitation, she started down the street after Nicole. Shoot or no shoot, she couldn't let Nicole out of her sight. If *Sassy* fired her, she'd have to live with it. She pulled down her sunglasses, yanked her sailor cap low over her forehead to disguise herself, and trailed Nicole and the kidnapper.

Esme kept them in sight by keeping her eye on the parrot, who was easy to spot, sitting up on the guy's shoulder. She followed carefully as Nicole, the man, and the parrot turned a couple of corners, then hurried toward one of the seedier-looking piers. The sailor stopped outside an old shack, then looked around. Esme ducked behind a trash can. When she looked up, the sailor was gone.

"Nicole!" Esme cried into the stiff sea breeze. But her voice was drowned out by the squawk of the gulls. To her horror, she watched Nicole peer into the window of the shack. But instead of fleeing to the safety of the crowded street, Nicole darted around the back. Esme took off after her. She didn't understand what was going on! She reached the building in time to see Nicole jump on board a large blue-and-white yacht.

"Nicole!" Esme yelled again, but Nicole had already vanished down the hatch.

Esme hesitated. She was afraid to leave Nicole alone. What if that creepy sailor should find her? Esme squared her slender shoulders and gingerly stepped off the pier onto the deck of the boat. No one seemed to be around, although there was an odd drilling sound coming from the bow. Esme would not let Nicole out of her sight until help came along. Some vague voice inside of Esme wondered exactly how help would come—or who even knew that Nicole needed help. But the sound of footsteps approaching the ship, sent Esme scurrying. She ducked down the hatch after Nicole. "Nicole?" she started to call, then clamped her mouth shut.

Not a moment too soon. The footsteps were now on the deck over her head, lots of them, and voices—loud ones, and scary ones, she thought. She looked around the dark hold. Crates were stacked against one side of the ship's hull. Esme hurried over and squashed herself down between two large boxes. As soon as the footsteps died off and the voices stopped, she would start hunting for her friend, even though she hadn't the foggiest idea where Nicole might hide on a boat like this. In fact, Esme didn't know a thing about boats. She generally avoided them, preferring dry, solid land. But to find her friend, she'd explore every corner of this ship if she had to.

A blaze of sunlight burst down into the hold as the hatch opened. Esme held her breath. Two sailors clattered down the stairs. Someone above deck threw down a couple of heavy sacks, and the sailors stowed them in a corner with much grunting and groaning. Then, they tossed some empty burlap bags in Esme's direction. When the bags landed right on top of her, it was all she could do not to sneeze.

While Esme was crouching in the bottom of the *Starry Night*, Quinn and Alicia had already arrived in Key West. They had made it over to the *Sassy* headquarters, hoping to find Esme.

"Por dios!" Alicia exclaimed as the walked into the pink and white lobby of Key West's Coral Grove Hotel. The entire Key West police department seemed to be there.

"It looks like there's been some sort of major disaster!" Quinn exclaimed, her reporter instincts aroused. "At least something *interesting* has happened." She started to glow.

"I would not look so happy about that if I were you!" Alicia said meaningfully. "I have a very bad feeling about this."

"You're right," Quinn answered slowly. "I'm sorry." Then suddenly, Quinn yanked the sleeve of Alicia's yellow cotton-knit cardigan and pulled her behind the nearest bank of potted palms. "I have no idea what's going on, but I don't think attracting attention to ourselves right now is a very good idea. I mean, we don't want our parents getting calls from the Key West sheriff and finding out we're here!"

Alicia could only nod nervously. Just then, the sheriff walked by with a sandy-haired woman in tow. She looked completely distraught. To Alicia's horror, the policeman sat the woman down on a bench right in front of the girls' hideout. She clutched Quinn's arm and they both pressed back further into the palms.

"Now, tell me confidentially, Miss Wood," the sheriff said, lowering his voice. "What exactly happened to, now, what was her name—Amy?"

Beside her, Alicia felt Quinn's body stiffen. Alicia breathed out the softest of sighs. "Esme!" she mouthed.

Quinn nodded ruefully. "Wouldn't you know—all this commotion!" Quinn whispered, then put a finger to her lips and listened intently.

Miss Wood ran her fingers through her hair, and prefaced her remarks with the deepest sigh. "Oh, Sheriff Trebaye, Esme's a very reliable model. Right at the start of the shoot down at the marina, she had her makeup on and that original Paxton Lambert minisailor outfit. The break was over, and she was with Sandra and Jasmine heading toward the next location shot. Then, the girls stopped at a Coke machine, and when they turned around, she was gone. I—" Here the woman started to break down. "Why, if anything happened to her, I will just die. I will—"

"Now, now. I'm sure there's a reasonable explanation." The sheriff pulled a very large, red-and-white-checked handkerchief out of his pocket. He handed it to the chaperone and said, "I might be able to make this easier for y'all if I could ask you some questions." He produced a notebook and ballpoint pen. "Now, what was the girl's name, her whole name? I'll need that, as well as a description."

"She's blond—very pale, almost white-blond hair. And the biggest blue eyes you've ever seen, and she's about five-four, maybe a little more. She's only twelve years old, but could pass for fifteen."

"And her name, Miss Wood?" The sheriff said slowly and very patiently.

"Es—Es—Esme—Esme Farrell," the chaperone stammered.

"Esme Farrell." The sheriff ran his tongue over his lip and slowly wrote the name down, then stopped. "Hey, I met her the other day at the bus stop. A pretty girl. She was about five-foot-three, brown hair. But she didn't look fifteen. No way. I'd peg her for a very young eleven."

"Brown hair?" The chaperone shook her head firmly. "Esme's extremely blond. And what in the world was she doing at a bus stop?"

Quinn and Alicia didn't wait around to hear

any more. Carefully, they backed out of their hiding place and stole out of the hotel. "Esme's missing and that can only mean one thing!" Quinn declared, as soon as they were out of earshot of the police.

"She's found Nicole."

"And followed her."

"But how do we track them down?" Alicia asked, taking her first good look at Key West. "*Madre mia,*" she added. "There sure are a whole lot of people here."

Quinn figured quickly. "I'm sure Nicole and her dad are on his boat. Maybe Esme followed them there. Let's ask about the boat, and see if anyone's seen a girl that fits either Nicole's or Esme's description," she continued authoritatively.

Alicia and Quinn hurried down the street toward the docks. Alicia took one group of shops and restaurants, Quinn the other, and they asked all the shopkeepers if they had seen either Nicole or Esme.

Quinn had just about given up, when she spotted an old sailor with a parrot on his shoulder. He was unlocking the door to a restaurant called "Skipper's Victuals and Nauticals."

"Excuse me, sir," Quinn said, walking up. "I was wondering if you saw a girl here today, actually two girls. One of them has light blond hair and the other, well, she has brown hair, and is about my height—"

"And looking for Captain Christopher?" the sailor added, as he pushed back his cap and grinned at Quinn. "You must be from the same school. Do you work for the paper, too? I promised her I'd introduce her to the gentleman in question."

"Dirty Harry no gentleplum," the parrot interjected.

"So, you've seen her?" Quinn whooped, completely ignoring the bird. She frantically waved down the block in Alicia's direction. The parrot eyed Quinn in horror.

"Danger! Danger! Danger!" it cried. Then, "Fire! Fire! Fire!" The parrot squawked and buried its face in the old sailor's neck.

"Easy, Harry," Skipper murmured. "Something strange is going on here, but there's no fire." He eyed Quinn intently.

"I've found her, I've found her!" Quinn yelled as Alicia got closer, and then turned back to the sailor. "So where is she *now*?" Quinn was so excited she couldn't stand still. She hopped from one foot to the other, and grinned as Alicia ran up.

"This man has seen her?" Alicia asked. She recoiled slightly from the parrot.

Dirty Harry fluttered to Skipper's other shoulder, and extended his neck to peer around Skipper's head to stare at Alicia from a distance. "Danger!" he squawked again, this time a bit weakly.

"Yes," Quinn said slowly, frowning at the parrot. "He saw her a little while ago, I think."

"Well I did, but I don't know where she is now."

Quinn's smile faded quickly. "I don't believe it."

"Me neither!" the sailor said, puzzled. "She was so eager to meet Captain Whitcomb. I went to the office to find out if he was on board his ship, and, when I came out, she was gone." He turned his faded blue eyes toward the ocean. "And now, even if she does turn up, it's too late!" He pointed past the dock.

With a sinking feeling in her stomach, Quinn followed the direction of his finger. A large blue-and-white yacht was slowly making its way out of the harbor.

"The *Starry Night*!" Alicia exclaimed, sinking back against a wall in dismay.

"Yep. The repairs were done early, and now she's gone."

"She's on the ship?" Alicia asked, stunned.

Quinn shook her head. "*Ships* are 'shes,' Lish. He doesn't mean that *Nicole* is gone." Then she threw her head back and groaned. "But, I think you're right. I think Nicole *is* on that boat. If she was asking about meeting Captain Whitcomb, I don't think he kidnapped her at all."

"Kidnapped?" the sailor exclaimed, looking quickly from Quinn to Alicia. He narrowed his eyes suspiciously as he asked, "Hey, what's going on here? Are you girls in some kind of trouble?"

It was then that Alicia spotted the sheriff and half of the Key West police department headed in their direction.

"I would say that we are definitely in trouble now," Alicia murmured, looking grim.

Quinn followed her gaze and breathed out slowly. She hitched up her black jeans and smoothed her hair.

"Hey, Trebaye," Skipper called out loudly down the block. "I think you might want to talk to these here little girls."

The sheriff walked up, followed closely by Sarah Wood. He stared in disbelief at Alicia and Quinn. "Who are you?" he asked.

"Neither of these girls is Esme," Sarah Wood sighed loudly, looking more distraught.

"No, but we know her—and Nicole!" Quinn took a deep breath and bravely addressed the sheriff. "It's kind of a long story. You see, we're all from Palm Beach, and we followed Nicole down here because Esme saw her here last night. But we think Nicole's on that boat." She pointed to the *Starry Night,* which was now out well past the reef.

Alicia looked scared, and added in a small voice, "And Esme's probably with her!"

CHAPTER 12

The engines started up with a terrible whirr, and Nicole jerked forward. She clutched at the sack of potatoes on her right, trying to keep her balance and avoid tumbling headfirst around the dark hold below the deck.

A few more minutes! she told herself. *Only a few more minutes.* She had to keep still at least that long. Then the *Starry Night* would be safely out to sea. She'd be able to stand up and stretch, go above deck into the sun, and finally find her father. But until then, she was a stowaway—a stowaway who could be put off the ship and sent back home again.

Meanwhile, she tried to ignore the way the potatoes were poking her in the sides and back. Worse yet, she had to pretend that the weird gasping sounds coming from across the hold were nothing. Nicole was generally not afraid of the dark, or of most animals—but she was definitely wary of rats.

"UUUUUUUGHHHHHHH!" came the scratchy cry—it was right across the way!

Nicole's shoulders stiffened. Rats didn't make sounds like that, people did. Was there another stowaway in the hold? Whoever it was, Nicole didn't want to find out. Stowaways, especially in South Florida waters, were usually bad men who smuggled guns and drugs. Nicole was beginning to feel very scared. Now, all she wanted to do was find her father. With her dad, she'd be safe at last.

As the boat began to rock on the open waves, she cautiously began to stir. In the dark, she focused her eyes on the small sliver of light that filtered through the trap door leading to the deck. Hugging the shadowy floor, Nicole crept toward the steps.

She heard someone cry out, "OOOOOOOOHHHHHHHH!" It was followed by a breathy sneeze.

Nicole turned around quickly and shook her head. It couldn't be, she thought, not here, not now.

"Esme?" she whispered incredulously.

"Niii—Ni—Nicole!" The groan was unmistakable. "Oh, Nicole, you're here. You're alive. They haven't killed you yet!"

Before Nicole could begin to respond, a burlap sack came flying in her direction, followed by a bent, blond-headed shape. "Oooooooooh, my stomach!" Esme's moan was terrible to hear. "I'm going to be sick!" she wailed.

"What are you doing here?" Nicole demanded, planting her hands on her hips and scowling. Esme couldn't see her face in the dark, but Nicole didn't care.

"Saving you—" was Esme's muffled response. "But I'm going to be sick, all over this outfit. It's a sample from the new Paxton Lambert line, and if I mess it up I will never, ever model again. I'll be—" Esme burped. "I'll be blacklisted forever! Ooooohhhhhhh!" She moaned again.

"You are about to ruin my entire life!" Nicole cried. "And all you can think about is your dress!"

Esme didn't respond. She stumbled over to the steps and flew up them with remarkable speed, considering the fact that she was wearing heels and that it was pitch-black in the hold. She pushed against the hatch. It sprung open in a burst of light. Esme tumbled onto the deck. Strong arms grabbed her, as she ducked her head over the railing and was terribly, painfully, miserably sick.

"What's going on here?" a loud voice demanded.

Despite the pitching of the boat, Nicole flew up

the steps two at a time. "Dad—oh, Dad!" she cried and flung herself into her father's arms.

"Who are these little girls?" another voice asked.

Nicole looked up. It was her father's new first mate. She recognized his picture from a magazine article. "I'm Nicole Whitcomb," Nicole managed to croak out, holding back her tears. "I'm here to see my father!" She clung to her father's sleeve for a moment, then straightened herself up. She didn't want to embarrass him in front of his crew.

"And who's *she*?" her father asked, stunned, pointing toward Esme, who was dangling limply over the rail. Two sailors were holding her up.

Esme finally managed to show her face. "Hi—" she greeted Nicole's father with a weak three-fingered wave. "I remember you," she stammered, as she clutched at her stomach and turned perfectly green. Then, she started rambling, "You're Nicole's dad—I'm her best friend, Esme. We met at a Christmas play a long time ago. I think I was five then. I came here to save her from being kidnapped!"

The information was so startling that Captain Whitcomb had to sit down.

"Nicole?" He looked at her, and at the same moment motioned for his first mate to come over to him. "Blair," he commanded, "I think we'd better head back into port. We're probably going to put in again for a couple of days."

"But Dad!" Nicole started to protest until she saw the stern expression on her father's face. She moistened her lips and lowered her eyes.

"Now, men," Captain Whitcomb continued, "see if you can make Esme feel a bit more comfortable. I'm going to take Nicole down to my cabin to talk for a little while!"

A few minutes later, Nicole was sitting on her father's bunk. From the sounds of laughter up on deck, she could tell that Esme was already feeling better. A ship full of very handsome sailors sure could work wonders, she thought ruefully. Unfortunately her own hurts weren't so easily cured.

"Now, Nicole," her father said softly. "Let's hear the story right from the beginning. Exactly what are you doing here, and does Diana know where you are?"

Nicole shook her head. "She wouldn't care either!" she said petulantly.

"That's not fair, Nicole. She cares about you more than anything in the world," Captain Whitcomb replied firmly.

"You're just saying that because *you* don't want me either," Nicole blurted out. She couldn't believe how childish she sounded, but she also couldn't control her feelings any longer. She was too upset and had been holding it in for so long.

"Anyway," she cried, "now she's got Jonathan to worry about and doesn't need a perfect Miss Preppy like me!"

With that, Nicole threw herself on the bed and began to cry, her thin shoulders racked with sobs. Her father touched her back awkwardly. He hadn't seen his daughter cry for a very long time.

When Nicole had calmed down a little bit, her father murmured slowly, "I don't know what to say. . . ." He swallowed hard, and looked as if he were at a total loss for words. Then, thinking for a moment, he added, "Who in the world is Jonathan?"

He sounded so baffled that Nicole had to look up. She actually started smiling through her tears.

"Oh, Dad," she said and threw her arms around him one more time. "Then, you *don't* know about the wedding after all!" she cried, gratefully accepting a wad of tissues and blowing her nose. She explained about her mother's upcoming wedding, and about Adam, and how he was bald and had this terrible son who had already been kicked out of three schools. Nicole was getting very excited as she tried to explain everything at once. "And I don't belong there with them!" she cried out. "I belong here." She flung her arms open and pointed out the porthole. "With you—in the middle of all this."

Her father grinned as he stammered, "Maybe you do. . . ."

Nicole's heart soared. But it quickly sank again when he added, "Someday. But not now, Nicole. I can't take care of you now. This is no life for an eleven-year-old girl."

Nicole hung her head and was quiet. "You're right, of course," she said finally, because he was. She knew it deep down inside.

"That doesn't mean I don't love you or want to spend time with you. I couldn't help any of the problems that cropped up this Christmas, but I see now that I should have planned to see you—experiment or no experiment. And perhaps," he added after a pause, "we'll check what we can do legally to change our visiting arrangements. I really think we should see more of each other."

Nicole was glad he said that.

"But, as for running away," he continued seriously, "that was more than wrong. It was inconsiderate. Your mother, your grandmother, and grandfather must be very worried." Her father proceeded to scold her soundly for causing a lot of grief.

They talked for a little longer before he got up and placed a ship-to-shore phone call back to Palm Beach informing Mrs. Whitcomb that they were coming home.

As the *Starry Night* pulled back into the harbor, Esme was thrilled to see the commotion on the dock. "Look, Nicole. It's like a welcome-home parade!" She bounced up and down, and waved happily to the crowd. Her dress was rumpled and her hair was a hopelessly tangled mess. Esme didn't care. Kesia spotted her first, then Sarah, and the models' photographer Ken. "Wow! They're not even angry with me!" Esme cooed, and favored the two nearest members of Captain Whitcomb's crew with her best cover-girl smile.

Nicole tried to smile too, but the sight of the squad cars and the photographers made her knees go soggy. "Oh, Esme, I have never been so embarrassed in my whole life."

"Embarrassed?" Esme scoffed. "Enjoy it. This is your moment in the sun." Esme squinted through her sunglasses, and that's when she spotted Quinn.

"Nicole!" Esme shrieked. "Quinn is here, and so's Alicia. They came all the way from Palm Beach to rescue you." She turned toward Nicole and confided happily, "That was after I told them you were kidnapped by that strange man with the parrot."

"Oh, Skipper!" Nicole said his name with such affection, Esme did a double take. Then she spotted Quinn, and the smile froze on her face. Quinn looked furious. Beside her, Alicia was jumping up and down. *"Que Bueno!"* Alicia cheered.

"You're back, Nicole," she shouted over the crowd. "You're back!"

A few minutes later the yacht was tied up onto the pier. Captain Whitcomb led Nicole down the ramp, and went right up to the sheriff. Quickly, he explained what had happened.

"That's good news," Sarah Wood commented, looking on. She waved a stern finger at Esme, as she warned, "Young lady, if you ever behave that way on a shoot again, you will never model for *Sassy* or any other major-market magazine."

Esme looked contrite, and muttered, "Sorry, Miss Wood." Then she looked down at her clothes. "Shall I change my dress now?" she asked in a very small voice.

"Sure," the photographer said as he walked up. "Then we'll just touch up your makeup and I think we might finish shooting right down here. I like the locale," he continued, narrowing his eyes against the sun and framing up imaginary pictures with his hands. "Yeah. I'll ask the captain if he minds us using his ship for background."

He searched the crowd. "Makeup!" he barked, and a short dark-haired woman rushed up. "Get her into the next outfit and fix her face, please," Ken commanded. "And do something with her hair."

Before they whisked Esme away to the trailer, Quinn caught up with her. Nicole and Alicia were close behind. "Next time, Esme, don't pull a disappearing act like that," Quinn almost yelled.

"Me?" Esme gasped. "It's Nicole who disappeared."

"Right—but you said you saw her kidnapper push her into a truck, and then you just hung up."

Esme looked from Alicia to Quinn and said seriously, "Okay, I promise I will not do that again. Just—uh—" she covered her mouth and giggled, "leave you hanging."

Quinn let her knees sag in reaction to Esme's terrible pun. "Cornflake!" she called after her. "We'll make sure you keep that promise!"

CHAPTER 13

"Esme Farrell always lands on her feet," Quinn proclaimed. She sounded disgusted, as she knelt in the back seat of the rented Grand Am, watching Esme out the window. Even before Nicole's father had thrown his suitcase in the trunk and bundled Nicole, Alicia, and Quinn into the car, Esme was back at work.

The photographer was so taken with the image of the *Starry Night*, he had decided to shoot a whole spread on the dock in front of the blue-and-white exploration vessel. Skipper and Dirty Harry were hired to give the set more local color. As the car pulled away, Quinn saw Esme flanked by the old sailor, holding his bird and posing coyly for the camera. Behind the photographer, a crowd of very cute guys was whistling, grinning, and making fools of themselves, trying to attract Esme's attention.

"Esme's not the only one who's landed on her feet this time," Christopher Whitcomb commented dryly, as he followed the road onto the Overseas Highway for the trip back home. "I'd say all three of you did!" He paused to let his words sink in, then viewed Quinn and Alicia in the rearview mirror. "You could have all gotten into serious trouble—at your age, getting up and leaving home like that—and lying to your parents in the process." He paused before he added, "But you all managed to make it through—this time." He didn't exactly spell it out, but there was a hint of pride in his voice, too. They *had* made it through.

Alicia and Quinn sank down a little in the back seat. Before they left, Mr. Whitcomb had phoned both the McNairs and the Antonas from his ship. He planned to call them again when he got back up to Palm Beach, so they could pick up Quinn and Alicia from the Todd's. Quinn didn't relish the thought of her father's reaction to her little escapade. Alicia had already been informed that her allowance was to be cut in half, and that she was to be grounded for the next two months.

In the front seat, next to her dad, Nicole sat a little straighter. Her father was proud of her, she knew, and whatever happened at home she'd always remember that.

"Which does not mean, young lady, that all is forgiven and forgotten," Mr. Whitcomb said with a particular set of his strong chin that made Nicole wince. But the wink he gave her, while the other girls weren't looking, assured Nicole that everything was okay between them.

Nicole really dreaded seeing her mother again, but she hadn't imagined quite how bad the scene between her parents would be.

"I tell you now, Christopher," Diana Whitcomb threatened. "I am going to press charges against you for this." It was nearly midnight, and the three girls were waiting in the living room for Alicia's and Quinn's parents to come. No one was sure how, but the argument had broken out about five minutes ago, and for the Todd house it was an unusually loud one.

Mrs. Whitcomb paced from one end of the elegantly decorated living room to the other, and then back again. She stopped in front of the fireplace.

Christopher Whitcomb had his hands clasped behind his back. He was holding them together so tightly that from where he sat, Quinn could see the knuckles were white. "You haven't got a leg to stand on, Diana dear!" Nicole's father yelled.

He sounded so sarcastic that Quinn winced. She stole a glance at Alicia, who sat very still on the pale floral sofa, looking intently at her hands. She was at least as embarrassed as Quinn was. She wasn't sure how she'd ever look Nicole in the eye again. Nicole had always been so private about her family and whatever fights went on at home, and now two of her best friends were seeing her parents at their worst.

"I wish my dad would hurry up and get here!" Alicia murmured through clenched teeth. "Facing a death squad at midnight would be better than this."

Quinn had to agree. The last thing she expected when she reached the Todd estate was a scene. People like the Whitcombs and the Todds never had scenes. Or, at least they weren't supposed to. The argument between Nicole's parents was worthy of one of the sleazier episodes of *Dynasty*. Neither of them seemed to care that Nicole was in the room, or her friends, or Jonathan. Jonathan, meanwhile, was over in the window seat, and he was definitely smirking. Of course, Adam Stanton was looking more uncomfortable than anyone, as he sat perched on the arm of an easy chair, sipping a Coke. Quinn actually felt sorry for him.

"All these years," Mrs. Whitcomb continued to fume, "you've tried to turn *my* daughter against me. And now you lure her down to Key West—"

"Mother, he did not *lure* me anywhere!" Nicole yelled, shocking everyone as she jumped up.

Her face was tear-stained, as she faced both her parents. "I want to live with my father," she cried. "Don't you understand? I don't want to live here anymore!"

Christopher Whitcomb ran his hands through his graying blond hair. "But Nicole," he said, "you can't live with me. We've been through this a hundred times." He paused and looked sadly down at his daughter. "My lifestyle's not suitable for a girl your age," he continued slowly. "You need to go to school, have a normal social life. You can't spend three-quarters of the year on a boat sailing around the world."

To Alicia, the prospect of spending all that time on a boat full of adorable sailors sounded absolutely heavenly. But Quinn simply groaned, thinking of how much they would all miss Nicole if she left Palm Beach.

"Nicole has no idea what she wants!" Mrs. Whitcomb snapped suddenly, glaring at her daughter. "One minute she's into horses and becoming a . . . a vet—"

Quinn suddenly jumped up. "Stop it!" she shouted. She couldn't stand one more minute of this fight. "*All* of you!" She looked first at Mrs. Whitcomb, then Nicole's father. "The problem around here is nobody really *talks* to anybody. Nobody *listens*. Everyone's too busy being polite."

"Not tonight!" Jonathan Stanton mumbled

from the corner. Quinn silenced him with a furious glare. Jonathan shut up but stared at Quinn. She looked away first and quickly turned her attention back to Nicole's mother.

Diana Whitcomb looked Quinn up and down as if she were something lower than a bug. "How dare you get involved in this? Florence Hartman warned me about you. I will have you know, Quinn—Kelly—whatever your name is, that this is none of your business. It's a family discussion."

"This is no discussion, Mrs. Whitcomb," Quinn insisted. Alicia's eyes grew very big. "It's an F-I-G-H-T—fight," Quinn added, spelling out the word. "And it's about time you had one. It's about time you let your feelings out."

"Quinn!!" Alicia hissed in warning.

Quinn was too angry to listen. "Nicole ran away from home because *you* are getting married again. But you never even bothered to listen to how *she* felt about it."

Nicole spoke up softly. "No, Quinn." Nicole looked right at her mother as she said carefully, "I never told my mother how I felt about it."

Mrs. Whitcomb looked at her daughter as if seeing her for the first time. "No—" she paused. She moistened her lips and twisted the fine paisley fabric of her skirt between her fingers. "And I never asked. I wasn't around to give you a chance." Mrs. Whitcomb broke off and looked at

Quinn. An odd expression flickered across her face.

Adam Stanton cleared his throat. "I know this is all a bit awkward," he said, looking at Christopher. "But Nicole, I think we're all to blame for what happened. We should have broken the news to you in a different way."

Nicole eyed him suspiciously.

"Really," he continued. "We should have made you part of our decision, and helped you to adjust to the idea of getting a second father after all these years."

"It's just that no one really cares what I think," Nicole yelled angrily, as if this were the first opportunity she had ever had to tell her family how she felt. "I sort of fade into the woodwork, around here, back at school, everywhere. Nobody cares what happens to me!" Nicole added.

Alicia gasped. "That's not fair, Nicole!"

Quinn seconded that. "We care. We cared enough to risk being grounded for the rest of our lives just to go and find you in Key West when we thought you had been kidnapped."

Jonathan started to laugh. "Kidnapped? You really thought that?" He glanced at Quinn, amused.

Quinn tilted her chin in the air, determined to ignore him. She didn't know the first thing about Nicole's future stepbrother, except that she was sure she wasn't going to like him.

"From now on," Adam Stanton said quietly, "things will be different. Sometimes," he added, looking right in Jonathan's direction, "family crises like this are helpful. Quinn is right. It's good to get things out in the open, air our problems. Maybe Nicole can spend more time with her father, if she'd like." He turned to Christopher, who quickly nodded in agreement.

Diana Whitcomb bit her lip. Grudgingly, she gave in. "Nicole's old enough now for a different arrangement. Maybe you can spend part of your vacations with your father . . . on his boat. Maybe, sometime, you can even invite your friends along—Alicia, Esme—" Mrs. Whitcomb paused deliberately, the pleading look on her face asking Quinn to forgive her earlier outburst. "And, of course, Quinn."

Nicole's face lit up. "You mean that?" she exclaimed.

Her mother nodded. "It'll take some getting used to—the idea of you following in your father's footsteps!"

"His wake, actually," said Quinn, who always liked to use the most accurate word possible.

Christopher Whitcomb treated her to a smile. Then, the three adults started talking about possible visiting arrangements as they left the room.

"Quinn," Nicole said the minute they were gone. "I don't know how to thank you—for what you said tonight, and for coming to rescue me."

Quinn flopped down on the sofa and stretched out her long legs. "Well you *did* cause a lot of trouble," she said slowly, though her blue eyes were sparkling with mischief.

"I think congratulations are in order," Jonathan said, as he sauntered up to the girls and looked down at Quinn. "I didn't think Miss Perfect Preppie had it in her! There's more to you, Whitcomb, than meets the eye," he continued, as he grinned at Nicole. "You're pretty cool. Even *I* haven't managed to run away from home—at least not yet."

Quinn knitted her brow and turned on Jonathan. "Nothing's cool about running away and causing trouble. I'm going to be grounded for at least a month, and Alicia even longer. Running away from things is a pretty stupid thing to do."

Nicole started to defend herself, until she realized Quinn's sharp remarks were meant for Jonathan.

Jonathan shrugged. "Whatever you say," he said, winking at Alicia as he ambled out of the room.

"Is he *really* going to live here?" Alicia exclaimed, as she watched Jonathan wander down the hall toward the kitchen. She shook her head in disgust at the prospect, but her black eyes sparkled with interest.

"Worse than *that*!" Nicole moaned, and collapsed on the floor next to the couch. She wrapped her arms around her chest and uttered a miserable sigh. "He's going to G. Adams Prep next semester."

"Yuk!" grumbled Quinn.

"Oh?" said Alicia, craning her neck to catch one last glimpse of the good-looking rebel.

"Well, you win some, you lose some," Quinn commented.

"Tell me about it!" Alicia said sharply and pointed toward the picture window looking out on the circular drive in front of the Todd mansion. Headlights from two cars flickered off. Her parents and Quinn's dad had finally arrived to take them home.

"They're here!" Nicole sounded contrite. "I'm sorry, guys, for getting you in so much trouble."

Quinn grimaced at the thought of the family showdown once she got home, but to Nicole she said, "It was worth it. You've gotten that stuff with your parents sorted out."

Nicole's eyes shone at the prospect. "With a little help from my friends!" she laughed. "Even Esme chipped in!"

The girls started to giggle, remembering how Esme had gotten so sick, only to be instantly cured by the sight of all the handsome sailors.

"But, thanks to Jonathan," Nicole flashed Alicia a significant look, "I don't think things are going to be dull around here."

Quinn's eyebrows shot up. "As far as he's concerned," she said scornfully, "I think your problems have just begun, Nicole Whitcomb." Then the three girls walked slowly to the door, arm in arm, ready to face their angry parents.

Watch for **THE REAL SCOOP**
First in the Palm Beach Prep Series

"Help me!" Esme Farrell squeaked, as she clung to the rocky ledge.

"Hang on for just a little while longer," Quinn McNair yelled down, trying to calm Esme. "We've got a plan." Quinn turned questioningly to the other kids gathered around her.

"I have it!" Stephanie Barnes exclaimed.

"What?" Quinn asked eagerly.

"I go camping a lot with my family," Stephanie explained. "And my dad taught us to do this survival technique."

"Tell us," Quinn said impatiently. "The teachers are going to notice we're missing any minute now, and I think Esme's getting really scared."

"Okay, everybody," Stephanie began, looking at the others. "Give me all your jackets and sweaters. We'll tie them together really tight and make a clothing rope to send down to Esme. With all of us here, we'll be able to pull her up—no problem.

"Okay," Ryan called a little later, as he secured the last two jackets. "I think we're ready."

Stephanie told everybody where to stand and how to anchor themselves.

"Okay, Es, just tie this around your waist,"

Quinn instructed, as she dropped the rope over the edge. "Hold on tight, and we'll pull you up."

"Yeah, and keep your feet planted against the rock so you don't bang into it," Stephanie added.

"Come on, Esme, you can do it," Quinn urged, trying to sound confident. "We'll have you out in a minute."

"Okay," Esme answered shakily. "I'm ready."

Everyone took their places, and slowly began to pull the makeshift rope, hand over hand. Quinn was nervous as she quietly encouraged Esme to hang on with all her strength. After what seemed like forever, Esme emerged over the edge. Quinn grabbed her and pulled her onto level ground.

"Are you okay?" Quinn asked, hugging her friend.

"Now I am," Esme murmured. "Just totally gross and dirty," she continued, brushing the twigs and leaves out of her hair. Her eyes were swollen and her face was covered with dirt. Her hair was disheveled, and her sweater was all stretched out and filthy.

But Esme still looked worried. "You know, guys," she said quietly. "We have to make a pact not to tell *anybody* what just happened."

The kids all turned and stared. *Not tell anybody about the best rescue ever?*

"Please!" Esme begged. "I'm sure we wouldn't be able to take any more trips together. So, what do you say? Do you all promise to keep the secret?"

"Yeah," said Ryan, reluctantly.

"We do too. Right, Mimi?" Stephanie added.

Eventually, everyone else also agreed. But when Esme and Quinn were back on the bus, Esme realized she *had* to tell Alicia and Nicole.

"Esme, *Caramba*!" Alicia cried. "What happened?"

"You see," she began in a monotone. "I slipped down this cliff and I couldn't get up. Quinn, Stephanie, and some other kids rescued me."

"Esme Farrell," Quinn interrupted. "You are the world's worst storyteller. It was a fantastic rescue."

"If you think you can tell it better, go ahead," Esme snapped back. She just wanted to forget the whole thing.

"I'll do better than that," Quinn replied, with a dangerous gleam in her eye. "I'll write it down! We still need one more article for *The Real Scoop* and this would be perfect!"

"Are you crazy?" Esme yelled, loudly enough to cause some girls to turn around. "You promised not to say anything!"

"I never actually said 'I promise,' " Quinn argued slyly.

"Quinn McNair, you make me so mad!" Esme said, her face turning bright red.

"Take it easy, Es," Nicole warned, trying to

calm her friend. "But really, Quinn. She's right. Everyone would get in trouble if the teachers knew."

"But it would be the best newspaper article," Quinn explained.

"Promise not to," Esme pleaded.

"You have to," Alicia jumped in.

Quinn sat silently for a moment. It looked as if she had no choice but to promise not to tell. And that meant she couldn't write the story . . . didn't it?